DATE NIGHT WITH A CORPSE

By Sean Seville

Published by Franklin Publishers
Printed in the United States of America

For permissions, inquiries, or additional copies, contact:
Franklin Publishers
www.franklinpublishers.com

Table of Contents

INTRODUCTION

A personal journal can serve as a daily record keeper of one's most intimate secrets and detailed accounts. The words written inside of these digests are for the author's eyes only. A sacred documentation of everyday life told with truthful intent. Innumerable types of people are in possession of them. Ranging from little girls to college students. Astronauts, architects, and artists may want to cherish the day and remember all of the integral details.

Even mad men...

1ˢᵗ Entry: Recurring Dream

Dearest Diary,

Damn it all. Another abysmal awakening from lackluster slumber. Why do I continue to regain consciousness when it is eternal rest that I seek and crave beyond all else? My name is Reinhardt Droff. This will be my first official entry into my brand new diary. I used to own one during my childhood at approximately ten years of age.

It was primarily used for doodling. Much more than writing anything of substance. Meaningful documentation of important events in my life scarcely occurred. Here I am at 34 years of age, living such an unhappy, problematic existence. This is why I decided there should be a second attempt at implementing proper conduct with a diary.

My hope is that it might grant me some sort of catharsis. It's doubtful, but given my bleak disposition in life, isn't it worth a try? This plan did not include making a diary entry at 3:30 in the morning, but no time like the present. Am I right? There will be difficulty getting back to sleep.

Once again, I've been plagued with that infernal dream. Always consisting of the most nonsensical visions. In the dream, I find myself standing on a tilted hilltop. There are tall strands of grass as far as the eye can see. It's nearly impossible to take sight of the dandelions that are rooted throughout the land.

For some inexplicable reason, I always assume that all of this takes place in Switzerland during the summer months. The sky is blue with very few perceptible clouds. The sun is shining so bright. I'm forced to turn and face the opposite direction while under duress. Then I become unable to move from the exact spot that I'm standing on. It is there that I scream at the top of my lungs, but this bellowing is devoid of sound.

A lone mime shouting into a void of nothingness. Oblivion has found me, and I belong to it. A miracle occurs, and it's suddenly raining condoms. Yes, that is correct. A precipitation of prophylactics.

After a brief duration, the downpour finally ceased. At that moment, a copious assortment of nude women are frolicking about the hilltop. Swedish, Scottish, black, Japanese. They are all beautiful and carefree. Then he appears, the same maniacal brute that I had envisioned on a multitude of past occurrences. A husky individual that is most daunting due to his stature. His reign of terror is uncompromising and relentless as he flaunts his enormous sledgehammer. Meant as a form of intimidation and much more, he swings forth with all of his might. Caving in the skulls of every single one of those unsuspecting vixens. Eventually, the slaughter ends, and all of the women vanish.

The brute focuses his attention toward me. He marches forward. There seems to be an immense determination to end my life. I cannot see his face because it is always covered with a black mask. Only his eyes are visible.

A wide-eyed devil, indeed. After being approached by this lunatic, the setting changes. Instead of standing on a hilltop covered with tall blades of grass in the middle of summer, we're now wearing heavy winter coats in the dead of winter. The sky is dismal and gray. Every inch of that hill is blanketed in snow.

Finally, I regained my mobility. The brute and I sat down to drink tea at a nearby dining table that suddenly appeared. It was round and small, but it served its purpose. A waiter, this scrawny, yet well-dressed man with a villainous mustache, materialized out of thin air to serve the tea. Apparently, a blizzard is brewing, but this does not deter us from imbibing this lovely beverage, which is piping hot despite the rapidly falling temperature.

The waiter seems to wince before disappearing without uttering a single word. I'll have to complain to management about this imaginary waiter. His manners are piss poor, and he should learn a thing or two about proper customer service. He didn't bother to ask if we required anything else. Hopefully, he's not expecting a generous tip. He'll be sorely disappointed.

I'm a little flustered, but then I take a sip. I swear that it's the best damn tea that I ever had in my entire life. In a single instant, all is forgiven. The brute leans in, muttering about his dreams of Olympic ice glory. As he talks, I wonder, are we all just monsters chasing grace on a slick surface, destined to trip and fall?

Initially, I was upset because I desired to choose and claim one of those lovely ladies for myself before their inevitable annihilation, then never getting the opportunity to do so. However, this feeling of resentment transitioned to glee as the waiter returned with dessert. The brute had been served a single slice of olive oil cake, consisting of vanilla cream and roasted strawberry compote. He can have that shit. The waiter served me a piece of black forest cake with shredded chocolate, laced on top of whipped cream frosting.

Once we finished our dessert, I refrained from asking the waiter for a wine list, as I proceeded in pulling a buck knife out from underneath my chair. I vehemently rammed the blade straight through the brute's cranium. Much to my surprise, he didn't die. There's always the same sheer disappointment felt. He laughed before transforming into a little, white, fluffy bunny and hopping away.

All of the women returned and were frolicking about as if everything was perfectly normal. Only this time they're in the form of reanimated cadavers. These zombies were having the time of their afterlives. Before attempting to claim what is rightfully mine, I awoke. Why in the hell do I consistently have the same wretched dream night after night?

It would be nice to ascertain some answers, but I'm afraid none will ever be given. Uh, my headache has returned... I promise to write again soon.

Truly yours,
Reinhardt

2ND ENTRY: PROPER INTRODUCTION

Hola Señor Diary,

You must forgive the abrupt ending to my first entry. I continue to have these infernal migraines. The pain was excruciatingly bad. However, I feel that it is important to start this diary documentation off properly. This log will be an accumulation of my deepest, darkest secrets. Also, revealing a more sentimental side of me.

This will be exposed only to you. Consider yourself the recipient of privileged information. Let's see, I don't want to chatter for the sake of it, but there are vital facts that should be duly noted. Please forgive my impropriety. Do not mistake me for a rambler.

Personally, I despise those people. Contemplating and sharing, indivisible. To hear of such behavior coming from normal humans, it can be a little off-putting. Of course, I'm a far cry from being anything that can be construed as typical. Your existence is undeniably crucial.

I should begin from a much earlier stage in my life. Back in elementary school, the adults often referred to me as a peculiar child. When other children would stare at me with mounds of contempt in their eyes, I was compelled to bite them. Whether or not an arm or leg had been exposed, my teeth were meant to make contact. It's not that I'm enamored with biting down on chewy human flesh.

For God's sake, I'm not a cannibal. My very being is devoid of any fascination or compulsion in devouring people. There aren't any other explanations to give other than I felt at the time that those little bastards were getting precisely what they deserved. Throughout my childhood, I came to the realization that very few people were worthy of my respect. Society itself has labeled me a pariah.

I considered teenagers dispicable even when I was one. Such detestable, loathsome creatures. No matter how many wishes were made, none of those repugnant cretins would simply keel over and die. Parasites that are part of the human race should be exterminated. That's just more wishful thinking, I suppose. During my years of academics, science was a subject that I excelled in.

Biology, to be exact. The mere thought of anatomizing a human being gives forth a warm feeling of comfort. Disassembling structured masses of flesh and bone has always been as fascinating to me as it is alluring. Early on, at age eleven, I began to practice on stray cats.

This course of action managed to satiate my impulses and deep desire to work on human test subjects. I did not wish to find myself in police custody. Plus, I'm not exactly a fan of the feline population.

I loathe their abhorrent faces, bodies, hissing, and god damn caterwauling. The planet can make do with a few less cats in existence. My contributions and dedication to creating a world that will eventually become devoid of these walking furballs should've been immensely appreciated. At the time, I quickly accumulated cats as if they were baseball cards to be collected. They were hidden inside of a large toolshed at the far end of my grandparents' backyard.

Only on seldom occasions did anyone ever enter this shack. What pleasantries followed as I sliced and diced in the name of science, but it would be an outright lie if I didn't admit that these deeds were accomplished for my own sick, self-gratification. I'm quite aware that most people would perceive my actions as appalling. However, everybody has to have a hobby. My flippant attitude toward the matter cannot be helped.

May those cats burn... and some of them did. The joy that I felt in carving felines open and fondling their extremities is indescribable. I've always been a manic depressive, but it must be stated that during the period of my life when I played medical examiner to Puss Puss and the rest of those alley strays, I experienced some of the happiest and fondest moments of my childhood. There were fat pudgy cats that no longer required heads. I wished to alleviate them of unwanted baggage before ascending to Kitty Heaven. Many of them were still conscious during the process.

Besides, I didn't exactly have access to an anesthesiologist to assist me in my work. I'm incapable of relating to the majority of human beings that exist in this cruel world. I found this sentiment to ring true through my high school years, and even that of higher education. After earning my college degree and enduring eight months of internship at a prestigious business firm (Tacklon and Co.), I dutifully entered the world of high finance. Unfortunately, I wasn't anything more than a corporate crony in the making.

In my heart, I didn't want this. A promising career that was short-lived, as it came to a crashing halt. I'm a man that was born with a silver spoon in my mouth. I've always been extremely wealthy. Regardless, there were more than a few business opportunities (of the illegal variety) that have been utilized during my brief tenure as a stockbroker. I'll never understand why inside trading gets such a bad rap.

To phrase it simply, I never have to work again. Yet, I choose to work with the common man. Taking a job in the food delivery industry wasn't my initial course of action, although it does function in my best interest. My schedule, my rules, I'm my own boss. If I ever decide to engage in what could be construed as unethical business tactics, those will be my choices to make. No one else's.

Until recently, I lived in a luxurious penthouse condominium for years. A delightful location that draws you in with its alluring atmosphere. Large varieties of restaurants, bars, bright lights, beautiful architecture. Life in the city is grand, but after both of my grandparents died, I decided that it was time for a change of pace. So, I decided to move back into my childhood home.

Six years have passed since I last stepped foot inside this house, and virtually everything is the same as I remembered. Currently, my true motive for returning here escapes me. An unseen force compelled me to come back. I wanted to make this move with every fiber in my being, although it's entirely inexplicable. It is nice to have so much space to myself.

My previous residence had 3 bedrooms, 1 ½ bath, with a kitchen and dining quarters. A little small for my taste, but I managed to turn it into a suitable home. The house that I now own is a lavish, lofty structure that sits on 14 acres of land. Speaking of which, landscaping services are called in every other week to keep the grass neatly man-icured. There's an old swing set in the yard that I used frequently as a kid.

It's miraculously still intact. The house it-self has six bedrooms, 4 ½ baths, a large dining room, kitchen, rec room… You get the point. I'm pleased that both the attic and basement have been well-maintained. All of the furniture is older but well-manufactured, so it's built to last with the highest quality. Cabinets, sofas, dressers, etcetera.

They don't make them like this anymore. In essence, the antithesis of the poor, cheaply made furnishings of the present day. Crap is what it's called and will never be found inside of this dwell-ing. The brown exterior of this house practically functions as camouflage in symbiosis with the trees that surround it. What a lovely home, indeed.

Seclusion is the very thing that I desire most of all. The time had come to sell my condo, and I did so in haste. It's a buyer's market. What can I say? This decision did result in making a slight profit, but I didn't do it for capital gain.

In a small part, I missed my small town home. Not because of its insipid inhabitants, but the lack of. There is a small population here, especially when it's compared to the big city. Rural living is for me. There's so much more you can get away with in a place like this (legal or otherwise).

On another personal note, I've always loved playing with knives. Perhaps someone such as myself should never have been taught Kali. A Phillipino martial art that can create an expert at wielding knives, which I just happen to be. Keep in mind that martial arts are intended for defense only (ha, ha, ha). It is essential that I remember to take some pills that were prescribed to me recently, an antipsychotic medication.

I'm only joshing. It's pain medication to help fend off my chronic migraines. They've plagued me for years, but have become much worse during the last six months. I'd better get ready for work soon. Some of those bastards don't tip well.

It doesn't matter how quickly the food arrives. Those particular individuals should burn in hell forever. Anyone who doesn't understand this

can suck my slippery penis. My body is still covered with Crisco baking grease. I was playing a
game earlier. Better go in the shower now.

Until next time,
Reinhardt

3RD Entry: Breaking Up Is Easy To Do

Dear Diary,

My heart aches as I long for true love. This sentiment might seem to be in complete contrast to the man that was introduced in the first two entries of this log. Nevertheless, it's certainly what I crave to acquire with deep determination and will. Lucille Strutters, what can I possibly say about her? From the bottom of my heart, she's a first-class cunt.

Allow me to explain why I'm so spiteful, and filled with animosity. This highly explicable hatred consumes me. Most men consider Lucille to be an extremely attractive woman. A brunette with long, wavy, sprawling hair that surpasses the halfway point of her back. Long, thin hazel eyes that are slightly slanted.

Her gaze can be just as alluring as the call from a siren. It lures you, seduces you. Eye lashes that are full and flashy without being artificial. What a wonderful figure this woman is in possession of. It's unfortunate that Lucille's personality fails to be paralleled with her looks. A bedeviled, perplexing gal that is quite competent at causing distress, frequently. We had dinner last night in a swank little restaurant located in the downtown area of Lennox. It's a motor of a metropolis that never ceases to run. The most lively events that take place anywhere near my rural town happen to occur in this city. Yesterday was Lucille's birthday.

I thought that she might appreciate some fine dining to celebrate. Apparently, I was mistaken. As soon as we were seated inside of the establishment, she began to complain about the loud chattering coming from the patrons seated near us. The place was packed on a Saturday. What did she expect?

Instinctively, I would avoid such an outing altogether. However, this is what she fancies. At least, typically. The waiter did not return within three minutes to take our order, so Lucille began banging on the table in a not-so-subtle manner.

This crass behavior was followed by her calling out to our server.

Obviously, she's not from very good breeding stock (at least not mentally). I insisted that she should stop this egregious conduct immediately. Naturally, I found this horrid display intolerable. An embarrassment in my everyday life is what my so-called lady had become. Why couldn't she have a slight accident, such as getting hit by a car or falling down several flights of stairs?

Anything to put her out of commission for a while. Frankly, the prospect of her being put out of commission permanently is a much more appealing notion. Lucille ordered cod. After receiving her order, she said that the fish was too dry. The waiter took it back.

He returned with another dish of fish. Now the taste is too bland. The waiter took it back. At this point, I was confident that every single person from the kitchen staff spat on this cod. Even I couldn't blame them at this juncture.

Fish was brought out to Lucille again. Once more, this woman wasn't satisfied with the dish. She insistently stated that it tasted worse than before (I'm sure it did) and she wanted me to try a piece. Utilizing good sense, I refused. If that wasn't bad enough, Lucille decided that complaining to the maitre d' was the appropriate course of action to take. If she were going to engage in deploying such tactics, they could be done while being better dressed.

I'm not a fashionista by any means; however, those dreadful pointy lime green witch shoes didn't go particularly well with her abysmal blue ensemble. I wore a dark blue suit with a matching ascot and brown shoes. When the venue calls for it, I dress to impress. Alas, the same cannot be said for the company that I keep. That awful experience was prolonged by Lucille's complaint to management.

On the bright side, I was able to consume my food, completely devoid of the kitchen crew's saliva and mucus. After leaving the restaurant, we returned to Lucille's apartment. An unpleasant hovel in a middle-class neighborhood that she called home. I refer to it as atrocious. If Lucille had any decency, she would hire a part-time maid.

If I wished to be surrounded by squalor, right now I would loiter around the train tracks and share needles with the hobos. Actually, Lucille's place isn't that bad, but I just wanted the night to end already. When one grows weary of the days' events even Skid Row becomes appealing.

Then this woman had the audacity to ask me to sing Happy Birthday before eating carrot cake. I detest carrot cake. She couldn't possibly have some good taste and favor a different flavor instead. Clearly, that's too much to ask for.

I gleefully imagined shoving Lucille's face down into the cake, and holding her in place until she becomes incapable of taking another breath. Only then would my birthday wish come true. Back to reality, I sung the stupid song and served her a slice of cake. Suddenly, I lost complete control of my senses. There was an immense inclination for me to enter the kitchen. I couldn't explain myself.

After opening the dishwasher, I pulled down my pants and defecated all over the dirty dishes. Solid soft stool followed by liquid diarrhea. I utilized paper towels to clean myself, and then those were thrown into the dishwasher as well. Lucille waited for me in the living room, but she began to question why I was taking so long. I explained that as of late, my diet has been rather poor.

The birthday girl couldn't begin to comprehend what the hell I was talking about. Of course, it didn't matter. Once the deed had been completed, I placed a dish soap pod inside of the machine, closed the door and pressed start. Subsequent to doing so, I washed my hands. After all, I'm not a reprobate. Lucille entered the kitchen, and she wished to know what I was doing.

A grin appeared on my face. "Nothing at all. Just helping out with the dishes," I replied.

She told me that I'm the sweetest and embraced me with a hug. If only she knew the truth. For a moment there, I fantasized of reciprocating with a firm, forceful bear hug that would result in the breakage of every single one of Lucille's ribs. Instead of acting on a delightful whim, I decided to press the cancel button on the dishwasher. I told her to behold your dishes and my bold protest. The dishwasher was opened, revealing a foul, wet mess.

"Is that fecal matter?" Lucille asked.

"Indeed, it is. Now your dishes are as shitty as your personality, my dear," I replied.

My heart was filled with so much joy, as I jumped up and down. Laughter spilled from my lips like an open fire hydrant. Part of me wanted to sing. Then I informed the shrew that I was breaking up with her on this meaningless birthday. Over here, there isn't a maitre d' to complain to.

However, if he were here, I think he'd be on my side under the circumstances. Relief washed over me by what I had done, both mentally and physically. I was spiritually cleansed. A loud, shrill came from Lucille before grabbing a butcher knife off of the counter. An important rule of conduct had been forgotten.

Never break up with a berserk, hostile woman that is standing near kitchen utensils. Lucille swung the knife at me several times, but I managed to evade her attack and emerged from the kitchen unscathed. It wasn't over yet. She chased me out of the apartment and down the hall. I barely made it to the elevator.

When the doors of that lift closed, I felt completely liberated. It was a fantastic ending to a ghastly day.

Truly yours,
Reinhardt

4th Entry: My Quirky Little Impulses

Good morning Monsieur Diary,

Three days have passed since I ended my relationship with that horrid harpy. Lucille has been what some people would refer to as persistent. Personally, I consider her display relentless. She has been calling my cellphone often, even at odd hours of the night. Lucille wishes to get back together.

I don't have any intention of doing so. It's probably a ruse designed to exact her revenge. Actually, I'm a little stunned that Lucille believes I could possibly fall for such a tactless ploy. For shame, may she burn in hell. Regardless, I decided to play along.

Yesterday, I made an attempt to drive my point home. We agreed to meet for brunch. The liberty of eating beforehand had been taken, as my objective did not include getting together and having a grand ol' time. Lucille suggested a picnic. This notion couldn't be more perfect.

The day was bright and sunny. Clear skies with a cool breeze. I picked up that female scorpion in my fine automobile. A drop-top convertible, manufactured ten years ago. I own several other vehicles, but this particular car is the fastest, which makes it the most crucial to my plan.

Honestly, it wasn't much of a plan. It was more of a sinister deed. Lucille became inquisitive. She wished to know where we were going. I told her it's a surprise.

Can't say that was a lie. The car had been driven nearly fifty miles before reaching Onyx Forest. After informing the wench that we had reached our destination, the car was parked. Then we both vacated the confines of my convertible. I needed to stretch my legs.

Lucille had the decency to pack the picnic basket with numerous delectable sandwiches straight from the deli. All kinds of meat: bologna, salami, turkey and pastrami. They were all topped off with lettuce, Swiss cheese and cheddar. The appropriate condiments, such as mayonnaise and mustard, were brought along. For once, this hellspawn did something correctly.

We entered the forest, and I led her to the middle of nowhere. I'm familiar enough with this forest to know that hardly anyone ever goes out there. The forest sprawled beyond measure, a fitting stage for mischief. Out here, even your echoes get lost.The bat in the belfry began to complain.

Lucille stated that I'm not any good, and that I'm an imbecile for driving her out to No Man's Land and getting lost. Of course, I knew exactly where we were. Lies would be told if I didn't say that every moment this shrew berated me felt like heaven. It only justified my cruel intentions. My actions would not lay heavily on my conscience. Something that I'm devoid of anyway.

Ten minutes passed before the wildebeest began to show signs of calming itself. Then I engaged in an apology for my lack of intelligence. Slowly, I approached the senseless cow and assured her that the surprise set on her behalf is one for the ages. I told Lucille to close her eyes and keep them shut just for a minute. Then she shall truly be astonished.

After doing so, I began to sneak away. I crept as quickly as possible, stepping between dry leaves and broken tree branches that were strewn about the ground. Lucille asked if she should open her eyes now. I didn't dare respond as it would give away my position. Once the succubus finally opened her eyes, I was already well hidden behind a tree.

Just as I hoped, Lucille began to search for me. She ran in the wrong direction as she called out my name. Also using a few expletives. Apparently, my name has been changed to Miserable Bastard, which were the kindest words out of her mouth. Nevertheless, Lucille went on, meandering further into the woods.

I walked steadily back to the road. There wasn't any reason to hurry. The car had been parked in plain sight. In no time at all, I found my-self sitting securely inside of my convertible. It was only right for me to add a sense of dread to Lucille's plight. I revved my car engine up, over and over again.

Patiently, I waited until I could hear Lucille screaming deep within the forest. Running des-perately while attempting to find her way back to the road before I drive away. A tremendous feeling of achievement filled my belly with pride. A smile crept across my face as I stared into those black woods. I turned to face forward and drive away.

Then I froze in my tracks. It isn't impossible. For a moment I thought I was staring at a mirage.

Illusions brought on by intense levels of excitement and joy. Then reality reared it's ugly head.

Lucille stood directly in front of my car. She nervously chuckled while struggling to catch her breath. Then she jogged toward the passenger side of my convertible. An attempt was made to open the door. Fortunately, I had the foresight to lock it.

Lucille told me that I had her worried. Of course, it was all just a silly game. For all of the grief this woman had caused me, I was entitled to a little payback. Not to mention that the battleaxe attempted to murder me the other night. Lucille continued to stand beside the car.

I turned to face her. "Remember when I told you that I have a wonderful surprise for you?" I asked.

"Sure, I do," Lucille replied.

Then I released the brake and sped away.

"Enjoy!" I bellowed.

My laughter became uncontrollable while ob-scenities were spewed from this jackal that I left in the middle of the road. Lucille will never bother me again. Thank goodness that I managed to get my hands on one of those sandwiches, and leave it in the car before we entered the forest. These type of shenanigans can leave a man completely famished. Damn, that pastrami was delicious.

Until next time,
Reinhardt

5ᴛʜ Entry: Party Hard

Dear Diary,

I realize that this is a late-night entry, but I just came back from a party. Yes, can you believe it? It's about time for me to get back out there on the dating scene. The prospect of meeting someone special is such an alluring thought. Why not take a stab at it? Figuratively speaking, at least for now.

Two weeks have passed since the dissolution of my last relationship. Apparently, someone in the neighborhood passed out flyers for this evening's festivities. A celebration forged as a birthday blowout. Trevor Lanz is the devoted, loving husband who planned this event for his wife, Sherry. The flyer that I discovered in my mailbox had a heart printed on the lower end of it.

An abundance of glitter was spread over the invitation. It had taken about five minutes to wash all of that shit off of my hands. Regardless, I had to admire Trevor's dedication. Both he and Sherry must share a most intense, loving relationship. Frankly, I was a little jealous. Although, I never met this stellar couple before tonight.

I told myself if Sherry is hideous and it appears as though her face had been ran over by a tractor, then I won't be so envious after all. Naturally, I chose to attend the party as the well-dressed stud that I am. My attire is comprised of beige, tailor-fitted pants with matching loafers, and a burgundy polo shirt. The festivities are primed to commence at 7 pm. A decision was made for me to show up fashionably late at 7:45.

Due to the nightfall, I regrettably omitted the aviator sunglasses from my ensemble. Such a presentation would've been uncouth. The couple lives several miles down the road from my house. With so many acres of land between all of our homes, we're still regarded as neighbors.

Finally, I arrived at the front door of this inspiring couple's abode. Judging from the exterior of this house, it seems to have slightly fewer square ft. than my own home. This, of course, gives me a sense of superiority. The rustic blue paint job doesn't do these people any favors either. In my hands, I held a twenty-year-old bottle of Chianti Classico.

It is best to present a housewarming gift to welcome people to the neighborhood, although it turned out that this couple has been residing there for the past seven years. This is also a birthday gift. No harm, no foul. Meet and greet is not my forte, but I can play the part if the occasion calls for it. Less-than-stellar music was blaring at high volume.

After ringing the bell several times, the master of the house finally answered. The door came swinging open. Trevor introduced himself with grace, and I reciprocated. He's a man in his mid-twenties. Dressed as a tourist in his own hometown. In my opinion, he could benefit from a haircut. My hair is a far cry from shorn, but this gentleman resembled a surfer dude.

Subsequent to entering this dwelling, I quickly turned my attention to the décor, which happened to be atrocious. Dear God, the cheap K-Mart furnishings. There were a multitude of paintings hanging on the walls. They seemed to be renderings produced by an alcoholic carny. Whomever was responsible for these hideous abominations should be institutionalized immediately.

The quicker we get him off the street, the better. Many of the guests were loud and obnoxious. Unfortunately, I could smell a hint of vomit.

The odor emanated from somewhere in the living room. In an alternate universe, I could've been complimentary regarding the Persian carpets.

It's just that the owners should've contemplated shampooing these rugs about four years ago. Referring to them as dingy is an understatement. However, none of this is relevant. If the Lanzes prefer to live in squalor, that is their prerogative. Soon Trevor introduced me to his wife, Sherry.

An extremely attractive woman who is also in her mid-twenties. Her hair was down to her shoulders, neatly pressed. She wore a tight, pink blouse along with a skirt. It had a swirling pattern of miscellaneous colors. Much to my surprise, this ensemble went well with her white high heels. Despite being after Labor Day, I did allow it.

Obviously, Sherry enjoys breaking the rules. That in itself is a personality trait that I can easily admire. Alas, this lovely lady has poor taste in men and is already taken. After speaking with the lady of the house, it didn't take more than the first two or three minutes for me to realize that she's a rambler. This woman went on and on about nothing.

It couldn't have been more than five minutes that passed before I realized that Trevor had vanished from sight. What a cunning cocksucker! Sherry's own husband dumped her off on me, so I could be bored to tears. It became impossible for me to decipher the tales that she spun. Every word was incoherent drivel. Each syllable rang like a jackhammer against my skull. Her words didn't just irritate. They corroded.

Damn it to hell. I reached inside of my pockets. My medication had been forgotten, and I was in dire need. This woman's dump truck mouth has caused me a migraine. It was the equivalent of starting up a lawnmower, lying down on the ground, and putting your ear as close to the motor as possible.

So, it might've been abrupt, but a necessity. I excused myself and hurried off to a different part of the house. A panic attack ensued. Haven't had one of those in quite a while. The usual trouble breathing, heart racing, and eagerly craving a bullet to the head.

A short time passed, and I regained my composure. Captivating sights were on full display out in the pool area. From here forth, much of my time at this house was spent out back. The patio was decorative with ribbons, balloons, and a large banner that read: "Happy Birthday, Sherry!" The pool has been well-maintained.

First thing that I found appealing all night. Second, was an assembly of ladies around the poolside. I talked to several different women there.

However, the infernal babbling of these inept individuals was responsible for the worsening of my hellish migraine. Out of urgency, I hastily searched for the nearest bathroom.

After embarking on a short expedition through that massive house, I finally found one. I immediately entered and locked the door behind me. Straight to the point, I opened the medicine cabinet and rummaged through it. A prescription bottle had been discovered. It contained Vicodin, score!

Not quite as potent as my own medication, but close enough. Tonight seemed to be a bust. A complete waste of my time. Without a doubt, I regret my birthday gift to Sherry. The Lanzes deserve a cup of tap water at best. Not a fine bottle of Chianti.

Then I proceeded in doing what's expected of me. The neighborly thing, the right thing. My pants were already unzipped. I pulled out my schlong and urinated on the floor and inside of the bathtub. Don't think for a moment that I would leave without christening what appeared to be a recently installed brand new sink.

Everything was used as a urinal except for the toilet. Rest assured, I left that house with a smile. When it comes to the Lanzes, everything that they

did has been forgiven. Well, I tried my best to so-
cialize, but I'm tired now.

Nighty, night, Diary
Reinhardt

6ᴛʜ Entry: Perusing The Online Obituaries

Good morning Diary,

Everyone on this planet has the right to know what love feels like. That indomitable emotion that sets your heart ablaze and will ravage you in flames. Some of us have to dig deep for it. I made the decision not to work today. Usually, my shift is at night, but my aspirations will require the use of the entire day and evening.

A shift in priorities has occurred. Love is worth the hassle, and I'm ready to indulge. My computer will be the essential tool, utilized during this search. What exactly am I looking for? Who can possibly tame this wild heart of mine that beats with rhythmic passion?

Liasions of my past have never granted me any type of recourse from my loveless and pitiful existence. Cupid has yet to call upon me. Why have I been forsaken? How will this gaping hole in my soul ever be filled? That perfect match is out there.

With dedication, and prowess, my ultimate goal can be achieved. At first, I sat in front of my computer with dread. A tad overwhelmed. Soon afterward, these feelings subsided by thinking in a practical manner. What are the characteristics that I seek in a suitable partner?

To begin with, she must be drop-dead gorgeous. Someone that can keep my attention with very little effort applied. This indicates that she's heard of makeup. I do not wish for her to wear so much that she appears to be employed down at the Red Light District. However, attempts should be made on her part to keep me attracted.

Speaking of which, alluring attire is in conjunction with this sentiment. A lady who wears lovely dresses, blouses, skirts, etcetera, happens to be someone that I find far more appealing than a woman who goes for a night on the town dressed as though she's applying for a job at the loading docks. If she garners some level of intelligence, that is definitely a plus. Empty bubble heads, I can certainly do without. Chatterboxes that can speak endlessly without having to catch their breath, make me wish that half of the population had their tongues removed.

Silence is a precious commodity, worth its weight in gold. In my opinion, all ramblers should be executed on site. It should be duly noted that I'm not a selfish lover. I wish to hear about all of her needs and desires, but do not bore me to the brink of tears.

My lady should have some ambition. There is so much to accomplish in this world, and it's never too late. A partner who has the capability of making me laugh would be presenting an astounding personality trait. Most women that I've been associated with cause me to fantasize about strangling them, due to their belligerence, ignorance, and often off-putting behavior in general. Amittedly, the prospect of seeing spilled blood from these women excite me.

Nevertheless, I do my best to refrain from murder. Messy kills or even tidy homocides, such as strangulation, are rather uncouth. I'm not a caveman. However, I would be remiss by not mentioning that I do struggle with urges, but I have never partaken in such activities... As the attentive partner that I am, my lady will become the recipient of all the love and care that she'll ever need. As I turned on my computer, a flood of thoughts both heightened my senses once again with dread and apprehension.

My mind was racing, and suddenly it happened... an epiphany. Almost instantaneously, I came to a realization regarding precisely what I'm looking for. You could name any number of dating websites. None of them were meant for me. My attention was turned to the obituaries.

My adoring lady is waiting. Finding her was my task at hand. I searched minutely through each page. So many images of the recently departed, graced my computer screen. I read about the cause of death for each person, even the ones that I wasn't remotely interested in romantically.

Tragedy after the next. Some of these circumstances were surreal. Deaths that occurred during camping trips. There were boating accidents, falling scaffolds, and sometimes it was simply old age. A larger ratio of the deceased that I discovered were ancient.

Elderly individuals that died in their sleep. Boring, just plain dull. Reading about deaths that are caused by unnatural causes really is quite arousing. I know not to share these thoughts with other people. That's what you're here for, Diary.

Regardless, my meticulous search seemed to be for naught. There were too many men, and obviously, I'm not looking for them. A few deaths of children were documented as well. Before giving up completely, I thought to myself that these are the most recent.

Scrolling back to last week's featured cadavers, might provide more successful results. Sighs came forth as I continued my exhaustive search. An utter waste of time. I only had two pages left, and that was it. Going back any further would be moot. If I did find a suitable candidate, she would've been buried too long without enough embalming fluid left within her body.

While checking through what few listings were left, I finally struck gold. A most fascinating obituary, indeed. Gwen Trappenport is her name. A fetching woman with natural beauty. Long, wavy, raven colored hair.

She was of medium build. Died at age 29. This woman is of Irish descent. Went back to school to earn a doctorate in photography. Silly girl, with your exquisite looks, you should be in front of the camera, not behind it.

It must be stated that Gwen checks all the boxes on my list of requirements. Thank the heavens that she wasn't cremated. According to this date in the obituary, the funeral is scheduled for this coming Sunday, and today is Friday. Preparations must be made, immediately. I pride myself on doing things alone.

This time, some assistance will be in order. Only one man can help me with this predicament. Fortunately, he happens to be my best friend. Frankly, my only real friend. There's tons to do.

Goodbye for now,
Reinhardt

7TH Entry: Marty The Mortician

Hey there Diary,

I've been a busy little beaver. It was of the utmost importance that I paid my buddy, Marty, a little visit. He doesn't reside in Cretin Acres (which is where I currently live). The houses here are a little above his pay grade. Marty lives in Ashton Village. A thirty-five-minute drive from my abode.

I gave him a call. The humane thing to do. He knows that my desire is not to ever show up on his doorstep unannounced. Although, at the time of my phone call, Marty was still working, but he insisted that I come over, regardless. The Furhnam Funeral Home is where Marty clocks in for work.

At least in his profession, some of the parties involved don't mind waiting if he shows up late for work. Marty runs the only funeral home in the entire village. It's been his family's business for generations. It started with his great-grandfather, burying the deceased in cheaply constructed caskets. Charging outrageous prices.This type of business practice is not something that Marty follows. He believes in selling quality products for fair prices. His coffins are built to last. A true friend to the end. Standing at 6'3, some people find this mortician a little intimidating. Others find him peculiar for a variety of reasons.

We've known each other since high school. A melancholic presence is what Marty always presented himself with. On seldom occasions, I would see him smile. Typically, these expressions of happiness were associated with a new arrival at his family's mortuary. He would become giddy with joy after learning of someone's death in town.

Having a fascination with death is considered to be extremely morbid and unhealthy by most people. In fact, some would say that this is indicative of a severe mental disturbance. No wonder Marty and I always have such a wonderful rapport. I'm only joshing. Much like myself, the man is just misunderstood.

What the masses might construe as idiosyncratic behavior is perfectly normal for us. I do recall that back in high school, Marty used to play on the basketball team. A handsome fellow who had plenty of dates. The fairer sex tends to be quite fond of my friend's height. Some girls who dated him made claims about bizarre fetishes he was into.

Damned if I remember what they said. Honestly, things were going quite well for him before the incident. We were both in the same grade, and it happened to be our senior year. I was mentally and scholastically preparing for college. At the time, I couldn't wait to attend school outside of this place and get away as far as possible.

Just needed a change of scenery. It appeared that Marty's tall and muscular physique was good for something other than attracting girls. He earned a scholarship to attend and play for Columbia. This opportunity gave Marty some perspective. He wondered about various things he could do in life that didn't involve dressing and undressing cadavers inside of his family-operated business.

Columbia was on the lower end of my list of schools that I applied to. However, I did grow fond of the possibility of us both attending the same school. Then Linda came along. Another one of Marty's lovers. Apparently, one night during coitus with the girl, Marty became a little too frisky and bit Linda on her lips... down there.

Supposedly, he did it so hard that Linda required medical treatment. Help was sought and ultimately found at the local hospital. Her brother

Bill had discovered what had happened and decided to confront Marty at the funeral home. Facing Furhnam on his own turf turned out to be a horrible mistake. During the time of Bill's arrival, no potential customers were present, only Marty.

Bill walked in like he owned the place. With an aluminum baseball bat in hand, he made threats and swore at his sister's lover. Marty laughed and told Bill that he was busy and didn't have time for this nonsense. Instantaneously, Bill began to swing the bat at Marty. A struggle ensued, and the bat went flying out of Bill's hands.

Marty proceeded in beating his adversary senseless. However, that did not suffice. You don't just walk into Marty's place of business and attempt to manhandle him without facing dire consequences. My dear friend dragged a barely conscious Bill into one of the backrooms where the unoccupied caskets are stored. Marty pried the lid off of one of the lower-quality coffins, then threw the bastard right in.

Several punches were thrown by Marty in an attempt to keep Bill under control. Subsequently, the lid was reattached, and a nail gun was utilized to reseal the coffin. Fear couldn't possibly be more prevalent in that funeral home than it was on that day. Bill hollered as if he had been set on fire. Marty gave his enemy explicit instructions not to waste his breath yelling, because he would run out of oxygen much faster that way.

Linda's brother pleaded with his captor to set him free. Marty replied with a hearty, "No way, Jose." Due to the fact that this room is located on a lower level, it didn't matter how loud Bill's bellowing became. No one outside of the property could hear him. After a few hours had passed, Marty freed Bill from the confines of that casket.

The mortician warned this fool to never utter a word to anyone about what transpired on that day, or there would be hell to pay. Bill agreed, then scurried out of the funeral home like a lost puppy, trying to find his way home. Unfortunately, later that evening, Bill called Marty's bluff and contacted the appropriate parties. The authorities came for my dear friend and arrested him.

After conducting an investigation, Marty was eventually released from jail. The fact remains that Bill showed up

unannounced at Marty's place of work and assaulted him. Thanks to this technicality, the kidnapping charges against Marty were dropped. Nevertheless, this incident did cause an ill-fated outcome. Despite reading the final report on Marty Furhnam's ordeal and being officially exonerated, college admission officers at Columbia retracted their offer and revoked the scholarship.

On that day, Marty's fate had been sealed. He became destined to work at his family's business for the rest of his days. After the death of his father, as the only living heir, the funeral home is indeed, his legacy. In my opinion, the last surviving Furhnam is destined for greatness. He deserves better. Who knows what will occur in the future we seek?

I'll explain in my next few entries what has taken place during my visit with Marty. Give me an hour or two. I'm in dire need of my medication. At least I have one great comrade in this world.

See you soon,
Reinhardt

8ᵀᴴ Entry: Day Of The Funeral

Yoo hoo Diary,

Did you miss me? Forgive me for not getting back to you sooner. Last time I made an entry, my level of fatigue had affected my mind. Some of the previously mentioned times and dates may not be quite accurate. Nevertheless, my astounding accounts begin anew.

Late Saturday morning, I arrived outside of the Furhnam Funeral Home. A sizeable brown and gray building with enormous windows installed on the first floor. Normal-sized windows on the second level. There is a parking lot that is adjacent to the funeral home. This is also on Marty's property.

Everything is clean and well-maintained. The furhnams always liked to convey a simple message: Just because you're dead, it doesn't mean you have to be dirty. Such insightful sentiment, wouldn't you agree? Not only is this Marty's place of business, but he also happens to reside there.

His living quarters are on the second floor. His father died 18 months ago. Cause of death was a heart attack. His mother passed on many years ago. My dear friend functions as a sole proprietor.

The front door of the business had been left ajar. I went ahead and entered this cheery establishment. The first thing that captures your eye is the wall-to-wall red carpeting. Some of the windows have sketches of roses around the perimeter. In the main lobby for visitors, there is a brown oblong table and several lounge chairs.

The only other noticeable thing would be the exceptionally long white mantle. The walls in all the other rooms matched this color. White, bland, but at least the paint isn't chipped. There are a multitude of rooms where funerals can take place simultaneously if necessary. The first floor is quite spacious.

Dead bodies are kept fresh downstairs in the Furhnam's mortuary fridge. There is an additional room where corpses are taken to and prepared for funeral presentations. A storage room for coffins and other miscellaneous backstock exists as well. Bathroom facilities are present, and I can't forget the office. This is where Marty spends a lot of time making final arrangements with the bereaved.

The business does quite well, financially. Let it be known that Marty doesn't do it for the money, but for the fun of the game. There's something about burying a man six feet deep that causes Marty's eyes to light up. This puts a little zip into his step and makes getting out of bed every morning, totally worth it. Marty was currently inside of his office.

He was yelling on the phone like a madman. Apparently, his distributor delivered a batch of defective, poorly manufactured coffins. The material used is of low quality and beneath Furhnam standards. Through natural deterioration, weather conditions, and living organisms, a buried cadaver might be exposed to the elements in less than two years. This hardly makes these coffins, products that can be sold with an afterlife guarantee.

The conversation on the phone ended abruptly after Marty slammed the receiver down in frustration. He sighed before taking a shot of whiskey. A bottle of hard liquor was always stored in the bottom right drawer of his desk. In all fairness, Marty didn't drink too much. Liquor is merely used for medicinal purposes to alleviate higher levels of stress.

Once my presence was acknowledged, Marty welcomed me with open arms. Similar to myself, my dear friend found most people repugnant for one reason or another. Well, perhaps not to the same degree that I did, but he can see flaws often enough with humankind as a whole. Curiosity engulfed Marty's mind. He wished to know why my visit was of an urgent matter.

I explained to him in full detail how I had finally found my soul mate, and she is from the community of the recently departed. I've come to realize that the love I seek can never be found among the living. Everything I ever longed for is currently laid out in a funeral parlor, over a hundred miles away. Love, in its purest form, finally awaits. The service will take place tomorrow. Her burial will take place promptly afterward. Any additional elaboration with Marty wasn't necessary.

After all, this is his forte. He knows everything there is to know about death in its most natural and unnatural forms. There was a mild possibility that my words left Marty awestricken. I'm quite aware that my desires are not conventional by any means. What can I say? The heart wants what the heart wants.

Different, is one word to describe Marty, but my best friend could've easily become judgmental and told me that I've lost my mind. This did not occur. Quite the contrary. Marty seemed to be pleased that I've finally stumbled upon love in any form. He agreed to help me with my dilemma.

There are several obstacles to overcome. The first of which is to acquire the lovely cadaver after her burial plot is filled. It is of the utmost importance that we wait until nightfall. Tomorrow cannot arrive soon enough. All of the relevant tools required are packed inside the back of my pickup truck.

I have a blue tarp that is large enough to drape over all of my precious cargo. Although a van would be preferred, I think it might be a little too conspicuous in case we are in the vicinity of law enforcement. It just might grab their attention slightly more than a small pickup truck. Once the body is exhumed, the open grave must be fully restored and refilled with dirt. It must appear as though the gravesite was never disturbed. Love may be eternal, but secrecy is survival.

No one will come looking for her if she isn't believed to be missing. After we bring my lady back to the Furhnam Funeral Home, this is where Marty's expertise is really going to come into play. Excitement showered over me in pure unadulterated bliss. An in-depth discussion ensued, ironing out all of the integral details pertaining to other phases of my plan. Obtaining love is not always easy. Sometimes, it takes a little initiative and a lot of work. In this case, manual labor (digging). We made preparations for our trip. Packed a few sandwiches and drinks. Marty doesn't have any memorial services to host over the next couple of days, so closing up shop will not present a problem.

Driving on the open road for hours on end is not necessarily a bad thing. Taking in the sights along with the atmosphere almost seems surreal. I've continuously added to this particular diary entry as this journey unfolds. I want to remember also savor every moment of intrigue, excitement, apprehension, and joy.

It is now Sunday morning. We were traveling for quite some time. An overnight stay at a motel was required for rest. The big day has arrived, but the monumental event takes place later tonight. My mind is completely devoid of regret.

All of my hopes and dreams will come to fruition. I'm certain that victory shall be achieved. Happiness comes once in a lifetime for some people. Maybe twice, perhaps never. In my lady's case, love will present itself in the afterlife. Eternity is a long time. My actions on this day prove that it's never too late. Hours have passed since my last written words. It's been dark for a while. We just entered the town of Camburg. Here is where I'll find her.

I'll write again soon,
Reinhardt

9ᴛʜ Entry: A Consideration Of Taxidermy

Hey there Diary,

Marty and I finally arrived at the Camburg Cemetery. The pitch black night surrounded us without a soul in sight. The gate that surrounded the grounds was left wide open. So, I drove the pickup truck inside, without incident. This scene is exactly what you would expect.

Infinite rows of tombstones were lined up. Some are made of granite. Others were derived from marble. Names on memorial plaques go un-noticed. At least, that's my opinion. They're not the easiest things to read.

In some cases, moss begins to grow over grave markers. If the cemetery grounds are un-kempt, inscriptions on plates can become illegible.

The grass in this graveyard could certainly benefit from some mowing in many areas throughout. Marty and I walked, searching for nearly thirty minutes before stumbling upon what seemed to be a freshly set mound of dirt. I knelt before a tombstone that read: Here lies Gwen Trappenport. Beloved daughter gone much too soon.

The truck wasn't parked that far away. I went back to retrieve it. After returning to the gravesite, I got out of the truck, then grabbed a couple of shovels from the back. Marty and I began to dig. My goodness, it must've taken over an hour to reach the girl's coffin.

If the dirt hadn't been placed there recently, it would've been much more difficult to remove the soil. I gently tapped on the casket.

"Hello, is anyone in there?" I asked.

I'm so silly. Where on earth would she be going this late at night? Nowhere, except with me. Slowly, the lid was lifted. Then I took a peek.

There she lay in slumber. A beautiful angel from Heaven above that's been buried down below. Violins were playing in my head. The moment I laid eyes on that decomposing beauty, I knew she would be mine at any cost. I tied the end of a rope around my lady's waist.

After vacating the grave, Marty and I pulled the cadaver from her burial plot. She was gently placed in the back of the pickup truck, and covered with the tarp. Once we did

that, the burial plot had to be refilled after reclosing Gwen's empty casket. Diligently, we worked. I spread the dirt smoothly over the top after we finished.

Honestly, I think we did a better job than the groundskeeper. Marty threw the shovels in the back of the truck. Oh dear, I certainly hope that he didn't hurt Gwen's head. We got inside of the truck and embarked on the second half of our excursion. My turn to sit in the passenger's seat. With haste, Marty revved up the engine and then drove like there's no tomorrow. He was just tired. Slumber is what he craved. I admit that I also shared this sentiment.

Due to the special cargo in the back, staying at a motel was out of the question. Marty and I took turns driving through the night. Only stopping to eat and use the restroom. This roadtrip served a unique purpose, and I shall remember it for the rest of my days. Eventually, Monday evening, we returned to the Furhnam Funeral Home.

We unloaded Gwen from the truck, then brought her inside through the rear door. This is the same entrance, utilized whenever cadavers are delivered here for business. My lady was well wrapped inside of the blue tarp. The time was only 6:38 pm, but exhaustion had overwhelmed Marty, immensely, and understandably so. He told me that he'd see me in the morning.

Without dinner or a shower, Marty went straight to bed. The tarp and its contents had been stored downstairs. My stomach growled with extreme intensity. I entered the kitchen after washing my hands and made myself a couple of sandwiches. As I sat there eating like a starving squirrel, I decided to wait and open the tarp as if it were a gift on Christmas morning.

Only a few hours to wait, and I didn't have to leave cookies out for Santa. That has to be good for something. Subsequent to finishing my meal and showering, I went to bed. No one had to say a word. Although good things come to those who wait, am I right?

Obviously, the following day would be much more exciting than the last, and it was indeed. On Tuesday at 11:04 am, I had awakened. Marty was already in the kitchen preparing breakfast. After brushing my teeth, I crept downstairs to the low-est level. Ms.Trappenport had been stored in the embalming room.

I eagerly anticipated making her acquaintance properly. With care, the cadaver was unwrapped.

What a stunning beauty. I picked out one hell of a prize. During her lifetime, Gwen usually had a ghostly pale appearance.

Now her complexion was more of a grayish tone. A cloudy overcast before the storm. Only a select few, after their mortal cessation can maintain such elegance.

Effort had been applied as I managed to lay her out on one of the steel tables without any assistance. Her body was cold, but I held her hand to give warmth. I lifted Gwen's eyelids, and what I observed in those deadpan eyes was love everlasting.

The texture of her face became rough. Not quite like sandpaper, but it's getting there. Applying a little lotion can go a long way. After this brief application, I gently stroke Gwen's hair. Then I assured the girl that she would smile once more. I lovingly gave Gwen a kiss on her forehead.

Fleeing on foot, I vacated the embalming room and raced upstairs. Is famine rearing its ugly head again? Indeed, it is. Thankfully, there is plenty to eat in Marty's kitchen. Breakfast was shared with my best friend. We had quite an interesting conversation over bacon and eggs.

Marty felt that filling Gwen with more embalming fluid at this point would be moot. She was already rapidly decomposing. His opinion is that the bastard mortician, originally enlisted to take care of Gwen, didn't give the final injection of embalming fluid in a timely manner. My objective has been explained thoroughly. This woman must be preserved at all costs.

Marty determined that the best way to do this was to subject Gwen to taxidermy. If performed properly, she just might last forever. The problem is that Gwen's flesh is already deteriorating. A minute examination had been conducted. Alas, in Marty's expert opinion, Gwen's decomposition has already gone too far for the procedure.

Woo! She certainly has a strong odor. Maybe that's the scent of love. I wasn't ready to give up hope. None of it mattered. Ms. Trappenport and I are meant to be.

Taxidermy is supposed to be my salvation, isn't it? If Gwen is going to rot, then we'll do it together. Destiny has made us one.

Good day to you,
Reinhardt

10TH ENTRY: HONEY, WE'RE HOME

Greetings Diary,

Marty provided me with all of the advice he could give. Ultimately, it's up to me now. My decisions, as well as my discretion, will determine exactly how this road is paved. We're in it for the long run. My will cannot be thwarted.

Back at my house, I kicked open the back door while dragging my lady, lovingly in my arms. Gwen had been wrapped in the blue tarp again, but once we set foot inside of my home, that cover was unraveled rather quickly. The cadaver rolled out onto my living room floor. I swear that woman giggled. We were going to have a grand ol' time.

Can you believe that we're actually here? The two of us together just as the Grim Reaper intended. This is an example of how sometimes death is a blessing in disguise (If you believe in that sort of thing). The house was locked up tight. I carried Gwen upstairs to the bathroom, then drew her a bath.

This is what you would refer to as an attentive lover. Although, I'm getting a little ahead of myself. After undressing Gwen, I placed her inside of the tub. I'm confident that my lady love found the water with added bubbles most soothing. She's been through so much.

Relax, my dear. You're home now. These are the words I conveyed, over and over again. The events of the last few days have been taxing on us both. Only through care and understanding can we make this work.

Gwen is like an undead doll. Her eyes were open but rolled to the back of her head. A slight grin crept to the edge of her lips. I reached into the bathwater. The temperature was just right. Set properly to Gwen's request.

Handfuls of bubbles and soapy water were flung into the air. A most majestic scene. Did I truly have the right to be happy? It's seldom that I ever experience this emotion. Having a glum and morose disposition is what I've become accustomed to during my years on Earth.

Money has always been accessible, but it has never been enough. Who would've guessed that happiness is only a grave robbery away? I could see the emotion in Gwen's eyes after they were rolled back into place. The subtleties of a caring relationship will not escape us. For I intend to give it my all.

My lady was eventually pulled from the bathtub and brought into the bedroom, where I dried her off, thoroughly. Gwen would've done it herself, but she was dead tired. Ha, ha, ha! Look at me, Diary. My sense of humor has returned. What a glorious feeling.

Gwen weighs about 125 pounds. Her figure is astonishing. In advance, arrangements were made for my darling to receive a brand new wardrobe of clothes. Gwen's measurements were listed in the obituary, which is highly uncommon. Nevertheless, the finest attire has been picked out by expert fashionistas.

This woman deserves the very best, and she shall have it. Gwen decided to wear a lovely, tight-fitting brown blouse (which accentuates he curves) along with a matching skirt. Can't forget the panties. After all, she's a lady. The blue flats suited her well.

Gwen admired herself in the mirror for a few minutes before allowing herself to be whisked away. I picked up and carried my lady love downstairs to the den. We both sat close to each other on the sofa. I gazed ever so lovingly into Gwen's eyes. She is so witty and keen. She made me laugh as we talked for hours. Despite Gwen's attempt to earn a doctorate in photography at the time of her death, many pursuits have been made. Did you know that at one point, Gwen secretly desired to become a veterinarian? She possesses such adoration toward animals. The thought of treating the sick and making them well appealed to Gwen very much.

The more this woman spoke, the more that surprising, vital details of her extraordinarily short life were revealed from those extremely chapped lips. Honestly, this is something that I find rather unsightly and unbearable to look at. Momentarily, I interrupted our conversation and hurried off to the bathroom. The medicine cabinet contained a necessary utility for one's proper presentation. Promptly, I returned to the living room and greeted Gwen with open arms.

I apologized for my abrupt departure. Then I applied the chapstick to Gwen's lips with haste. To say that her lips were extremely desiccated would be an understatement. A bottle of wine was opened earlier to celebrate our union. I dipped my finger tips into Gwen's glass of wine, and then rubbed them across her lips.

Liquor used as a moisturizing agent for the moment

turned out to be a useful tactical solution. A combination of both wine and the chapstick, caused those lips to become luscious. Darn it, I did forget to reapply Gwen's makeup after her bath. A light application will suffice. Not a heavy load. I do not wish for my dear woman to resemble a bar-gain-basement streetwalker.

Of course, this can wait until tomorrow. It's been a long day. Much to my astonishment, Gwen hardly touched her glass of Chardonnay. It's her personal favorite. I suppose she was no longer in the mood to drink.

Gwen felt slightly fatigued and wished to re-lax. She stretched out on the couch. After remov-ing her flats, I began to give my lady a foot mas-sage. The rigor mortis can make you a little stiff. Gwen told me that I am kind for doing this.

It's nice to feel appreciated for once. Gwen also thanked me for her brand-new, extravagant wardrobe. My lady must be seen in style, not rags. Anything less is virtually barbaric. Before I came to realize it, the time was 11:30 pm.

The hours flew by in a haze. We didn't have dinner yet. At this juncture, my lady love must've been famished. I gave an apology before walking off into the kitchen. It is customary that someone with vast wealth would have a cook employed to prepare dishes for him or her, but this is not how I operate.

I placed a couple of well-seasoned porterhouse steaks inside the oven. Soon we will sit down in the dining room and indulge in delight. What a lovely evening we have shared. This first night together has been nothing short of magnificent and magical.

I just checked the oven. It appears that the food is ready to be served. The dining room has already been prepared. Well, I am certainly famished, and my lady awaits.

I'll write to you again, soon,
Reinhardt

11ᴛʜ Entry: Whirlwind Romance

Dear Diary,

It's an amazing feeling when you're in love. Come to think of it, I've never been in love before. A brand new experience. Life is full of them, I suppose. Today I sat behind the keys of my grand piano. Revisiting this lost element of myself was nothing less than exhilarating. This hasn't occurred in so long.

All of those lessons were taken for years. They did help to create a more than adequate pianist. Dare I say, superb? Only if truth shall be told. Grandmother once believed that one day she would observe me playing at Carnegie Hall.

This dream of her's never came to fruition. My greed and ambition guided my fate, opposed to talent. Still, the notion of playing at a national level in front of enormous crowds is something to relish. Alas, during my adulthood, I've had very little inspiration for playing at all. Now I have found one.

Romantic ballads were played. One after another. Gwen sat in a sofa chair that is contiguous with the couch. She was in a partially slouched position. My darling's head hung to her far right.

Good thing that she's dead because that looks extremely uncomfortable. It didn't matter. Any chances of Gwen suffering neck pain is doubtful under the circumstances. Perks of the afterlife, I suppose. Although, my lady couldn't hold back the joy that she felt. A smile presented itself from ear to ear.

Gwen could hardly contain herself any longer. She asked me to continue playing. Gwen managed to make several requests. Anything for this lovely girl. Every single one of those songs was played with elegance and grace, as they should be.

Several tears fell from Gwen's eyes. It is my belief that this woman feels as strongly for me as I do for her. Destiny is sometimes fulfilled when you least expect it. As a photographer at heart, Gwen's desire was to take photographs, and that we did.

She was able to take a terrific shot of us while we were sitting at the table. We leaned toward the food that had been served during brunch. Gwen has a sweet tooth, so I had various pastries delivered. It turns out that she's partial to vanilla rose garden cupcakes. My lady must be more careful.

She got frosting on her pretty frock. I did warn her beforehand. There will not be any visits to the dry cleaner today. Therefore, the stain will settle. Believe me, I wasn't completely negligent. Club soda was applied to the affected area.

Rapid dabbing is the correct method to use, but the stain currently remains perceptible. A visit to the dry cleaner is imminent. We engaged in so many activities today. Without any rational reasons whatsoever, I gave Gwen a piggyback ride. I ran with her through the kitchen and dining room.

Then I gently let her down on the couch. She laughed as I bombarded her with a barrage of tickles. My lady told me to stop because she wished to be serenaded. Assurance was given that I'm not the most talented singer, and she may be gravely disappointed. Gwen didn't care in the least.

Effort that is given means more to this woman than anything. I did my best. Truth is, I am a decent singer. This was a mild attempt at me being humble. What a strange feeling that humility invokes.

I won't be doing this again anytime soon. Lack of candor has never been one of my deficiencies. Time passed before we entered the rec room. I decided to paint a portrait of Gwen. All of the required supplies were already at my disposal. My lady posed for me in a most lewd and provocative manner.

Since this is what she wished for, I was happy to oblige. Gwen was stripped down to her panties and brassiere. Those incredible legs were only slightly parted with a hand covering her crotch. What a naughty girl, indeed. My easel stood in an upright position with a fresh blank canvas readily available.

Paint cans were open and brushes prepared. The work began right away. This gorgeous gal is the perfect model. The art rendered must do her beauty justice. I've been known to dabble in painting projects, but art is not my forte.

Three hours later, I presented Gwen with the portrait. She began to frown.

"That doesn't look like me," Gwen said.

I told her that I did my best. Suddenly, I was approached by my lady. Then she whispered into my ear. Gwen told me this is all we can ever do.

It warmed my heart that my darling could be so understanding, even in the face of great disappointment. She asked me for another cupcake. I informed her that this will have to be the last one. It is important for my gal to watch her lovely figure. Hastily, I walked into the kitchen to obtain another cupcake.

Once I returned a minute later, Gwen took the cupcake from me and ate it in a hurry. My mind filled with apprehension. I'm now becoming privy to a more gluttonous side of my lady love. Is this a sign of things to come? No, of course not.

I had to remind myself that this woman is dead. If anything, Gwen will lose weight as she begins to wither away. This is something that must be avoided by all means necessary, but we'll cross that path when we come to it. So far, Gwen's looking relatively well. Although, her flesh appears to have a little more greenish color today.

In all of the excitement, it completely slipped my mind. Then I suddenly remembered. I scooped up Gwen right away, and carried her downstairs into the cellar. Arrangements have already been made. A long steel table was set up. I laid Gwen down on top of it.

Large unlabeled cannisters were contiguous with the work area. These tanks contained embalming fluid. Thin tubes with extensive length were attached. Gwen was hooked up and injected immediately. If I don't wish for my lady's flesh to falter, she must receive her injections periodically until a more permanent solution can be made.

I might require Marty's assistance for taxidermy soon, despite Gwen's current condition. Cannot give up hope. This woman belongs to me now, and even the gods themselves are powerless to take her away. For the moment, Gwen's body has been restored. The day flew by, but the night is still young.

Until next time,
Reinhardt

12th Entry: A Night To Remember

Hey there Diary,

Last night was one for the ages. If I recall correctly, I ended my previous entry by informing you that Gwen was in dire need of more embalming fluid. The mandatory injection of this precious substance occurred without any blunders. My lady has been made whole. Her appearance is astounding.

She glows with a heightened level of confidence that was previously unforeseen. Gwen's grayish complexion shimmered under the fluorescent lights. To me, she had never looked more radiant. Promptly, I dragged Gwen back down to the embalming room and placed her on top of the steel table. Vital awareness of my lady's rigor mortis is

essential. Her body has become more progressive-
ly stiff with each passing day.

Due to my highly attentive and nurturing manner, Gwen is given the type of massage that is desperately required. Flexing of the limbs will also help to provide Gwen with more mobility. We certainly don't want her stiffening up on me. Ha, ha, just a little humor.

After I completed the obligatory rubdown, my lady's muscles and limbs were much more loose, or as much as they can possibly be in this predicament. Thanks to the application of massage oil prior to my deed, Gwen's rotting flesh glistened and appeared healthier than ever. The oil contained minerals that soothe and ultimately moisturize skin of various types. Of course, the creators of this product did not have cadavers in mind. Regardless, prejudice of any kind will not be tolerated in this house.

After dressing Gwen, I carried her upstairs to the den. This is where we played a stimulating game of chess. Naturally, I defeated my lady, but one has to admire her astuteness and passion. Effort was gallantly given. However, it was all for naught.

The little lady is looking forward to a rematch in the near future. A bottle of wine had been opened over an hour ago. It's always best for it to breathe, before one indulges. I swear that this particular white wine, possessing a fruity aroma, is juxtaposed with a hint of salty bitterness, providing an exquisite flavor to cherish.

Apparently, Gwen is a fan. She already finished her second glass. Later on, we sat in front of the fireplace, where the heat from the flames warmed our bodies. Well, at least mine.

I read out loud some of my lady's favorite poetry. The author's name escapes me. Catching sight of the glimmer in Gwen's eyes is simply stupendous. I'm an entertainer at heart. Shortly after, I resumed my piano playing for about twenty minutes.

The sounds that I produced were a delight for Gwen's ears. How could they not be? Magic is hidden in the form of melody. My masterful ability to play is second to none. Eventually, I tired of this.

In a less-than-subtle manner, I transitioned to playing my old records instead. Tango music blared from the speakers that had been built into the walls. I slowly approached Gwen and stretched out my hand.

"My lady, may I have this dance?" I asked.

My heart skipped a beat when she accepted my invitation. After pulling Gwen out of her seat, I dragged her all across the dance floor. This delicate being's dancing is divine. We twirled around. Similar to loose umbrellas that are caught in the wind.

This woman is a pure delight. I can't remember the last time I felt this much enjoyment. Have I ever? For the life of me, I do not recall. Dancing can lead to fatigue sooner than usual when you have to drag your partner the entire time.

A flood of emotions came crashing into my psyche. The woman of my dreams is actually here in reality, and mine for the taking. We stood before the fireplace and engaged in a passionate kiss. At that moment, I knew that Gwen felt exactly the same way about me. When picking up a cadaver, it's always important to lift with your knees and not your back.

I carried Gwen upstairs to the bedroom. A trail of rose petals were spread across the floor. They lead directly to the bed. My romantic prowess dominates the scene. A nightstand is located on each side of the bed.

Lit candelabras sat on top of each one. Gwen was a little tipsy from drinking so much. I gently laid her down on the bed. The window was ajar. This allowed the breeze to take effect.

The sheer white curtains moved slightly with the influx of air coming from outside. As I lay beside Gwen we resumed our kissing. Then she tried to stick her hand down my pants. Before I realized it, my clothes were off. Gwen wished to conduct a little striptease for me.

After removing all of my lady's clothing, it had become apparent that the putrefaction of her corpse was slowly taking place, despite the injection of embalming fluid. Of course, this method is only meant as a temporary solution. What is also noticeable, even with Gwen's clothes on, is the unbearable odor. Well, I didn't purchase all of those overpriced fragrances for nothing.

Gwen was sprayed with one of her favorite perfumes. Then our intimacy progressed into full effect. I diligently performed cunnilingus with my lady love. What wonderous flavors the vaginal region retains after death. It's enough to make an ordinary man vomit.

However, I am anything but common. Momentarily, I thought my lady had an orgasm. But alas, the substance excreted into my mouth was nothing more than purge fluid. It damn near caused me to choke. Subsequent to spitting maggots out of my mouth, we moved on to coitus.

So much passion was involved. Quite some time passed before Gwen really had an orgasm... Fool me once, shame on you. Fool me twice... Damn purge fluid. It dripped from my penis after pulling out from the corpse. One thing is for sure, this will definitely be a night to remember. Thanks for always being here.

Truly yours,
Reinhardt

13th Entry: An Inspiration To Us All

Dear Diary,

My lady love must truly be the most gorgeous woman in the world. Why would such a natural beauty aspire to be behind the camera, taking photographs, when she should obviously be in front of the lens? One of my obligations as a loving partner is to help facilitate the achievement of all my lady's hopes and dreams. They must come to fruition. Which is why I arranged a photoshoot with world-renowned photographer, Pierre LeFan.

His forte is shooting supermodels. Making them appear vulnerable but also fierce. Eclectic passion is expressed through his lens. They say a picture paints a thousand words. This is definitely the case when LeFan's expertise is at hand.

Pierre's portfolio is something to admire. Riveting shots that can create spellbinding imagery from the most mundane scenarios. A woman in the coffee shop, holding a cup of brew before her lips. Legs partially crossed. Wearing a hat with an enlarged brim.

This creates a slight shadow over her face. A white dress with a splash of black, here and there. It's not too short. A sufficient length. The shoes that she wears are impeccable. Black high heels with cross straps.

The floor of this establishment is checkered. Surprise! It matched the model's attire perfectly. This is only one example of Pierre's exquisite work. Gwen is a refined, radiant beauty that is more than deserving of such treatment.

LeFan arrived at my home at precisely 2:00 pm. I informed him in advance that only he would be allowed onto the premises. Absolutely no other outsiders. My privacy is to be respected. Since I paid Pierre almost double his going rate, there weren't any reasons for the photographer to complain about these slightly unorthodox circumstances. Typically, a client goes to LeFan's studio, not the other way around.

Pierre couldn't remember the last time he made a house call. It was certainly before he garnered any type of fame on the international market. The man is a multifaceted business owner, mostly in France. However, this entrepreneur's ambitious drive causes him to frequently travel all over the globe. Only last week, he did a photo shoot in Dubai.

The royal family paid an exorbitant amount of money for Pierre's abilities. Gwen's shoot will take place in the den. LaFan's lights and props were set up by the man himself. When the arrangement was originally finalized, Pierre requested Gwen's measurements. He wished to provide a wide assortment of attire that would be deemed appropriate.

Unfortunately, I could not submit an image of Gwen herself. Providing evidence of my lady's existence in the form of an e-mail is far from recommendable. Usually, Pierre has clients sign a waiver that allows him to advertise, using images from his photo shoots. Needless to say, I did not sign any such document. Finally, the den had been set up properly.

Tall white boards serving as a blank canvas stood in the background. This allowed LeFan to digitally add the desired scenery during post-production. It could range from a snowcap mountain, perfect for skiing, to a sandy beach in Jamaica. The time had arrived for Pierre to meet my darling model. Gwen waited eagerly in the next room.

I carried her into the den and sat her down on the sofa chair. Gwen was already wearing one of LeFan's astounding picks for the shoot. A period piece, red sack gown. This is the type typically worn during the late 18th century for formal events. I can still recall LeFan's immediate reaction.

"Sacre bleu, what is wrong with her? She looks dead," Pierre said.

I merely explained that Gwen has been gravely ill for quite some time. This is a last-ditch effort to bring some joy into her life before the end. His help is required to make this dream come true. Her ailment is terminal, and it's my duty to do what I can before the lord demands a recall on her soul.

Pierre genuinely bought that shit. He seemed to be content with my explanation and became sympathetic to our imaginary plight. Lefan was determined to convert Gwen's fantasy into reality. She will become a supermodel. Photographed by the best in the business.

Lefan was informed that Gwen's mobility had become nonexistent, and improvisation would be required. The clueless fool continuously barked at Gwen with the kind of demands he would make to his other models (that are actually alive). Look happy, pout, shake your fist angrily at God, growl like a tiger, etcetera. Of course, Gwen is incapable of doing any of these things on her own. My attempt at giving assistance was made.

At times, I would turn Gwen's head slightly to the left or right side, cross or uncross her legs, readjust her eyeballs when necessary, pull her dress up ever-so-slightly to expose a little leg. Only recently did I gain the ability to alter some of Gwen's facial expressions more effectively, molding her like clay. Now I can make her appear as though she's smiling. Well, almost.

Two hours later, the photo shoot ended. Hundreds of pictures were taken. Changing Gwen in and out of various outfits and costumes can be quite time-consuming and exhausting, to say the least. After the editing was complete, there were so many lovely images to gaze upon. The experience itself was quite exhilarating for Gwen.

I'm glad that she's been granted this incredible opportunity. What a memory to behold and treasure for the rest of her days. None of this could ever be if it weren't for me. A dutiful and amazing partner is precisely what I am. How else would you describe me? Altruistic, yes, that word does come to mind. Perhaps even saintly. Certainly, this is the best way to describe myself. The expression displayed on the face of Pierre LeFan tells me that this must've been the most bizarre photo shoot of his entire career. The signed contract states that

Pierre is to hand over both the camera and the flash drive that's in his possession.

He is to never speak of his time here and what has taken place. In advance, my attorney quickly provided an addendum to the contract in the form of a confidentiality clause. If Pierre were to violate it for any reason, let's just say, his business would become my business, and Lefan is a newfound pauper. Personally, I don't think he could handle that lifestyle.

As it were, I don't believe LeFan has any interest in gossiping about what occurred here, even if he could. It's been quite an eventful day.

Until next time,
Reinhardt

14ᵀᴴ Entry: The Incident With Gale

Hey there Diary,

There has been an interesting update since the last time I wrote to you. Do you recall the big photo shoot for Gwen? You should, silly. It took place only a couple of days ago. An unexpected visitor showed up at my doorstep this evening.

Whitherspoon, first name: Gale. It must've been around 5:30 pm when she knocked on my door. At first, I didn't recognize her. Ms. Whitherspoon brought to my attention that she is one of my frequent, recurring customers. Her words ring true.

I've been so preoccupied with meaningful things in my life, I completely forgot about the existence of this worthless dolt. There were many nights that I made deliveries to Gale's homestead. What on earth is she doing here? This is the question that echoed inside of my head. I always surmised that Gale had a little crush on me.

That crush turned into a full-fledged infatuation. Every time I delivered food to Gale, she would flirt talk. Then she would proceed in talking some more. The woman isn't bad-looking. One might actually find her attractive.

However, there is a problematic situation pertaining to her mouth. The issue is that it never closes. Gale is a goddamn rambler, and I can't stand it. If her talking would ever cease, she might become twice as attractive. Although people with her personality traits are incapable of being quiet. An unfortunate truth that I've discovered long ago.

Nevertheless, on this night, Gale insisted on talking to me. My fear was that she would help induce one of my excruciating migraines. I haven't had one in so long. Regardless, I reluctantly allowed this harpy to enter my home. Welcoming intruders and additional unwanted pests is hardly a gesture that I can easily make. The preservation of the world I so carefully crafted must be kept at all costs.

Still, presenting myself with proper decorum and grace is what the Droffs are known for, among other things... I told Gale to have a seat in the den and make herself comfortable. Gwen was currently relaxing upstairs in the bedroom. So, there wasn't any chance that Gale would see something that she shouldn't. Little did I know at the time is that this particular ship had already sailed.

Ms. Whitherspoon was already well informed. I offered Gale a spot of tea. After the lady accepted, I entered the kitchen to make preparations. Five minutes later, I returned to the den with a platter. It held a tea kettle and two cups that were already filled to the brim.

I sat the tray down on the coffee table and handed a cup to my uninvited guest. Before sipping, I warned Gale that the tea is scalding hot. She wisely heeded my warning and blew on the beverage several times prior to imbibing. We were both seated on the sofa when Gale began to speak. She informed me of her activities from two days ago.

While Gwen's photo shoot was taking place, Gale just happened to be in the neighborhood. However, this coincidence did not occur by chance. Unbeknownst to me, Ms. Whitherspoon began stalking me that very day. As you know, I haven't been to work in about a week. Gale became upset because she would order food every day, and I haven't personally made the deliveries in a while.

She wanted to know my whereabouts. In hindsight, I do recall one of the window curtains being slightly drawn back on the day of the photo shoot. I did not pay close attention at the time. I'm usually very vigilant. Of course, only an incredibly irritating, nosey individual with no life of her own could take advantage of this momentary lack of awareness.

Gale finished her cup of tea, then she requested more. Oh, how I fondly imagined throwing the scolding hot beverage in the harlot's face, but I didn't dare follow through with such pleasantries. Subsequent to pouring more tea, Gale told me that she got a good look at the woman being photographed. These words were not to my liking. Ms. Whitherspoon believed that the woman appeared to be deceased.

Such a notion didn't seem possible. However, something didn't sit right with her. Gale decided to sift through the online obituaries. Eureka! The identity of my lady love has been discovered by this intrusive, buzzing bee.

After this grim revelation was brought to light, Gale considered informing the authorities. I politely asked what prevented her from doing so. Gale placed her hand on top of mine, then told me that she would prefer to see me by her side rather than the state penitentiary. I smiled before ensuring Gale that she had made a grave error in judgment. Also, I was completely oblivious to Gale's feelings and intention toward me at the time.

If only I had known, proper precautions would've been taken.

"I feel the same way and would welcome an opportunity to reciprocate your sentiment by providing you with a lovely dinner in the city," I said.

Naturally, this was all a ruse. A steaming pile of horseshit, and Gale slurped up every word. Ms. Whitherspoon found contentment within this predicament. Everything was going according to plan (so she believed).

Gale assumed that she could easily manipulate and force me into a relationship with her. Even if her distasteful tactics of blackmail weren't being used, and I had never met Gwen, never would I ever have anything to do with another clueless, rambling chatterbox such as this. Frankly, I find repugnance in Gale's mere presence. I silently prayed that God would strike her down at that very moment. Damn, it didn't work, go figure.

Ms. Whitherspoon asked me if the dead woman was still here. I told her that the individual she had seen was not dead but ill. She arrived with the photographer and then left with him. Gale began to chuckle, and I followed suit. Although, I didn't find any of this remotely amusing.

The burdensome woman shot me a peculiar look.

"You're not a convincing liar. So stop trying," Gale said.

Then she gave forth a yawn. This is the fifth yawn in the last two minutes. Ms. Whitherspoon could barely keep her eyes open. I suddenly remembered that during one of my last deliveries to Gale, she described herself as a very lonely woman, and that no one ever came over to check on her. This news is very informative because now I know that she won't be missed.

The woman slumped over in her seat. Gale's eyes were closed, and her heart stopped beating. It just so happens that the tea Ms. Whitherspoon consumed contained enough arsenic to level an entire football team. Thanks for playing. Now I'll have my hands full with discarding the body properly.

Fun times ahead,
Reinhardt

15ᵀᴴ Entry: Stephan Returns

Dearest Diary,

What a development to quite the predicament. Up to this point, I failed to mention that I have an older brother named Stephan. He left home at an early age, probably at fifteen or sixteen. Always living life on his own terms.

As I previously mentioned, our family is extremely wealthy. Perhaps I didn't speak of this before, but my brother and I were raised by my grandparents, Leonard and Josephine Droff. For generations, my bloodline has had monetary means of immense proportions. As a ruthless financier, my grandfather arguably made more money than any other Droff before him. I misspoke, not arguably, he definitely made more.

Acquisitions were the name of the game. His company would invest, eventually becoming majority stockholders in other businesses, and engage in hostile takeovers, if necessary. Which happened to always be the case. Then these businesses are sold off incrementally. Don't think of this as a fire sale.

These companies are worth more in parts than remaining fully intact. Hundreds of job lay-offs occur as a result. That's just the way it goes. Insufferable vermin would protest outside of Droff Industries. The unions organized strikes on what seemed to be every other week.

This method of fighting back is moot. Why make demands if it's inevitable that you're going to the bread line? Nevertheless, my grandfather did not wish to receive so much negative publici-ty. Whenever this occurred, it caused Droff Indus-tries' stock to plummet tremendously. Nose dives on the market are never pleasant to watch.

Years later, my grandfather finally decided to retire. He had been diagnosed as having half a doz-en ulcers. The stress was killing him slowly. Droff Industries was eventually sold off for a staggering sum.

My grandmother, the certified bible thump-er, always read the scriptures. God this and god that. I mean, god damn! This sentiment did not rub off on my grandfather. In fact, his favorite sin was greed.

He once told me that the only reason my grandmother's babble was tolerated was because she had a great ass. How do you respond to a comment like that? Ofcourse, I didn't utter a word, especially since I was only nine years old at the time.

Stephan is more of a Lothario than myself. My representation of proper etiquette is always present. Although, as an antisocial deviant (of sorts), I sometimes fear the loss of social grace that is required in order to perform dramatically on a regular basis. This does not apply to Stephan. My brother is a highly skilled sociopath.

Yes, I know. Look who's talking. Nevertheless, I learned everything from him. His charming demeanor is used to con older women out of their money. Behaving as though he is smitten with his victims, and then convincing them to participate in impractical investments. Stephan doesn't require financial gain by utilizing such despicable tactics, but he enjoys engaging in heartless scams for the love of the art.

My brother makes some of these unsuspecting women believe that he owns a small business that is going under unless there is a last-minute investor who can save the day. Sometimes a "terrific opportunity" would present itself, and Stephan's lovers would have an opportunity to make some money. Once again, it would only require a small investment. I consider Stephan's conduct abhor-rent. It's shameful to lead these lonely hens into financial ruin for fun. Unlike what I do in the name of love. A conscience is what my brother is devoid of.

Then again, who am I to judge on the matter? I don't have one myself. Nor would I want one. What would I do with it? A conscience can only interfere with ambition. It hinders power, striving, and motivation to move ahead.

Allow the naivety of simpletons to drown themselves where they stand. You can throw them a life preserver, and they still wouldn't use it to reach the shore. Needless to say, grandmother didn't approve of Stephan's life choices. Apparent-ly, his way was not in God's plan. With every wak-ing moment, my grandmother went after Stephan. Constantly reading from the good book, which Stephan and I considered bad.

She attempted to get my grandfather in-volved, but he wouldn't hear of it. In fact, the old man was proud of Stephan. He encouraged my brother to bleed these women dry. Of course, these words were not spoken in front of his dedi-cated wife. Stephan idolized my grandfather, but he was always away on business trips.

Once my brother outgrew his infatuation with the old man, he decided to move out. The bible thumping became exceedingly worse as time went on. One day, while Stephan was in my grand-mother's presence, he denounced God and walked out the door with a packed bag, never to return, or so it seemed. My grandfather always had a soft spot for Stephan. He made sure that his grandson was very well taken care of.

Before my grandfather's demise, trusts were made for both Stephan and myself. We need not or have not. Just kidding, we have it all. I moved back home after my grandmother died. Stephan isn't the only one who considers the scriptures as intolerable. Nevertheless, the prodigal son has re-turned.

Another joke, he's worse than ever. Stephan showed up on my doorstep this morning, looking completely disheveled. Apparently, his latest wife threw him out with the trash. It turns out that she lacks appreciation for cheating spouses who forni-cate with their wives' best friend. When it comes to marriage, I suppose the third time's not the charm.

I'll give him credit, having every single one of those harpies sign a prenup is just good business sense. Besides, the documents were devoid of any infidelity clauses that would've sent Stephan to the poor house. Years have passed since our last encounter. We were never very close. Maybe this visit will signify a new beginning.

Another individual that lacks a conscience... Perhaps Stephan's timing is impeccable. We're still getting reacquainted. Stephan is going to stay with me for a while until he finds a suitable property to purchase as a new home.

He can assist me with getting rid of Gale's carcass. She's getting a little ripe already, and I refuse to waste an ounce of embalming fluid on this wretch. Don't worry, I won't write again until she's been dealt with.

Until then,
Reinhardt

16ᵀᴴ Entry: Good Riddance

Hello there Diary,

There's more than meets the eye when it comes to my brother. Since Stephan left home all those years ago, he's picked up a few nasty habits. The worst one happens to be sexual assault. That's right, ladies and gentlemen. My brother happens to be a serial rapist.

We were sitting in the kitchen having breakfast, and Stephan decided to make this admission as if it were completely normal. He describes a woman struggling, screaming, fighting him off as some kind of fetish. What a sick fuck. But enough about that. I still had a cadaver to dispose of.

I reluctantly informed Stephan of my unfortunate predicament. The man appeared to be stunned as I elaborated. This stark revelation came in the form of introducing Stephan to the intrusive hussy that needed to disappear. My brother was surprised to learn that I committed an act of murder. What was I supposed to do? Gale was an insufferable twat. The world is better off without her. His reaction only proves that he doesn't know me very well at all. Besides, he's a goddamn rapist. Who's he to judge?

It's true that this is my very first murder of a human being. Definitely, a worthy candidate has been selected. Much to my delight, Stephan offered to help discard this foul woman before I could ask. He apologized for not staying in touch on a regular basis. Then he gave assurance that he'll be there for me.

This sentiment struck me as peculiar coming from Stephan. He's arguably even more callous than myself. Family ties hold very little value to us both. Despite being away for so long, I could tell that Stephan had become much more ruthless than when he was a teenager. His aura glowed crimson red. A true villain if I ever saw one.

Intuition tells me that Stephan may have engaged in far more egregious activities than cornholing the unwilling. Why did he insist on staying with me for a while? What is his true motive? Does he have one? Nevertheless, I did require his assistance. Hopefully, his very presence here doesn't backfire in the near future. He mustn't bring unwanted attention to my residence. Obviously, I have a few secrets that should remain hidden. Later that evening, Stephan chopped Gale's corpse into a bevy of pieces. He worked as if butchering carcasses were his calling in life.

The bathtub became a suitable work station. This is surely Stephan's natural gift. I observed my brother as he hacked away at that harlot. He has such a refined technique. For the first time ever, I was proud to refer to Stephan as my kin.

Once the job had been completed, I noticed that the blade of my hatchet was dull. Blood dripped off the apron that Stephan now wore. He quickly removed it, then walked over to the sink and washed his face and hands that were also covered in blood. Coats of this sticky red substance stained every inch of the bathroom. It's as if the body had exploded.

I grabbed a mop, sponge, and lots of towels. My closet contained several large containers filled with bleach. Before cleaning, I stripped myself naked. Diligently, I scrubbed the entire bathroom. While this occurred, Stephan began to fill trash bags with body parts. My brother's assistance was invaluable. Not to mention, what a time saver. Subsequent to getting dressed, Stephan and I loaded up my truck with what can now only be referred to as compost. I remember glancing at my watch. The time was 11:40 pm when we got inside the truck and sped away.

I drove over to Drakken Lake. Sometimes the locals would leave small boats and canoes by the shore. We were in luck. A rowboat in excellent condition was tied to a post. I was confident that the owner wouldn't mind if we borrowed it for a while.

The boat was loaded with all fourteen of those heavy trash bags. Fortunately, every one of them remained intact as they were transferred from my truck to the boat. Once we were in the water, I rowed the boat slowly, as Stephan periodically dumped a bag here and there. That decayed matter sank down into the dark, murky unknown.

I heard rumors that an alligator was sighted here a few weeks ago. If there is any truth to this claim, this type of predator could help solve all of my worries. It's capable of devouring a large percentage of Gale's remains over time. Possibly all of them. Finally, the task at hand was done.

We rowed back to shore. I carefully retied the boat's rope to the post. A sigh of relief came from Stephan before entering the truck. As I drove home, my brother began to laugh. Did someone tell a funny joke that I'm not aware of?

The truth is, Stephan enjoys these morbid moments very much. There wasn't a soul around that lake. There couldn't possibly be any witnesses. My brother wasn't responsible for the death of this woman, but he behaved as though he had just gotten away with murder. Technically, he's now an accomplice.

I'm compelled to believe that this isn't his first rodeo. If Stephan hasn't killed before, I'm partial to $5 hookers. For the record, I am not. After settling in at home, I introduced Stephan to Gwen. She was sitting upright in our bed.

I used the fly swatter to kill some flies that were buzzing around her head. I forgot to turn on the air conditioner. Flies hate the cold. Stephan didn't say hello, which I found quite rude. In fact, he looked at me as if I had gone completely mad.

My brother simply shrugged his shoulders and smiled. Then he walked out of the room. Afterward, I made it clear to Stephan that if he were going to continue staying here for the foreseeable future, my relationship must be respected. Stephan sighed before speaking.

"Listen, we're both adults now. This is your business. I have a few fetishes myself. Whatever makes you happy, makes me happy. My intention is not to impede whatever it is that brings you joy. Hopefully, you're just as understanding when it comes to my kinks. You'll learn of those soon enough," Stephan said.

To say that my brother's words induced anxiety within myself is an understatement. My situation just became much more complex. At least I have you to confide in, Diary.

Thanks for always being there for me,
Reinhardt

17ᵗʰ Entry: Trouble In Paradise

Dear Diary,

I don't know what's gotten into Gwen lately. All of the bickering is unwarranted. Nobody likes a nag. Can I ever do anything right in Gwen's eyes?

Is my conduct really that unruly? She's been complaining about me not spending enough time with her. This claim of hers is utterly ridiculous. Maybe once in a while, I go out with Stephan to grab a drink, but that doesn't mean that I've become negligent.

Just this morning I washed her hair. Last night, she was given a sponge bath. Gwen is always kept in a nice air-conditioned room to help keep the odor under control. The peak time for rigor mortis has passed for Gwen. Tissue in her body is slowly breaking down thanks to bacteria and other enablers.

So, her flesh is becoming softer, more pliable. Now I'm having an easier time when applying lotion to the more chafed areas of her body. That's gratitude for you. A lovely flower-patterned blouse and turquoise slacks were what Gwen was presented with just a couple of days ago. I felt that this outfit would really bring out the color in her eyes.

In response, Gwen told me that she found the attire tacky and that my taste in women's clothing is abysmal. As of late, she has become more demanding. After giving Gwen a lengthy foot massage, she insisted on my redoing her makeup. Gwen told me that she did not wish to look like a rodeo clown and that I am capable of doing a much better job.

There are more extensive tales I could tell. The stress became so overbearing that I quit my job in the food delivery service. Then one day online, I came across an advertisement. A gentleman is seeking help for the home care of his elderly, handicapped brother. He happens to live six miles away.

Past experience in the field is not required. The applicant must be prepared to tidy up a little. The job description includes having patience and spending time with an ornery old man. If he doesn't like you, you'll be fired immediately. If by some miracle he connects with you, then the job is yours to keep. I've never been in the home care business. Aside from Gwen, I always considered the prospect of taking care of others, revolting. However, for whatever inexplicable reason, this job listing appealed to me. Also, I was in dire need of a distraction from my home life. Perhaps during these few hours away at work, Gwen will have some time to reflect and come to a realization regarding her wrongdoings.

Never take a good man for granted, or me. It was the day of the interview. I drove out to this enormous estate that rivaled my own in aesthetics. Unfortunately, looks can be deceiving. Only the exterior of this home appeared to be in immaculate condition.

I parked my car before getting out and traversing the cobblestone walkway that led to the gray villa. The grass is neatly trimmed. The property sat on acres of open land with very few trees. These people must be very wealthy indeed. After reaching the front door, I rang the doorbell.

There appeared to be crows nesting high up in one of the trees, and several were stationed on top of nearby telephone wires. Some people would consider this to be an ominous sign. Poppycock! I could never be disturbed by such trivial superstition. The door before me opened. Standing there was a man, tall in stature. Well dressed in a black suit and tie.

I was invited inside. After entering the abode, this man introduced himself as Dansforth Tollington, brother of the impaired. This individual is responsible for placing the online ad. He did not live in the house. Only his brother resided there.

My eyes took full stock of the surroundings. In an instant, anyone could see that the owner of this home is a hoarder. Miraculously, the man isn't living in complete filth and squalor. An employed attendant comes by once a week to ensure that the owner's possessions are kept as neat and presentable as possible. Order must be maintained to avoid the authorities from stepping in and issuing citations.

Copious amounts of newspapers were stacked a mile high. Infinite piles of clothing were set in rows. At least they were neatly folded. Boxes filled with old 8-tracks and cassette tapes were mounted wherever room could be found. Shelves loaded with books, both read and unread.

Knick-knacks of all kinds were strewn about. Most of which did not clutter the middle of the floor. Fragile curios sat inside numerous glass cabinets. The house itself consists of six bedrooms, four and a half baths, a kitchen, a drawing room, a second den, a dining room, a basement, an attic, and even a pool out back. Although it has been completely drained and covered with a tarp.

It's official, this house is bigger than mine, which I do find irksome. Dansforth and I took the elevator up to the second floor. Then we walked down the long corridor. Located at the end is the bedroom of Dansforth's brother. This is where I met Herbert.

He's a mean buzzard indeed, but somehow we seemed to mesh. Herbert isn't exactly incapacitated and certainly not bedridden. However, he does have a little trouble walking. That's what the cane is for. Herbert is capable of taking care of himself, for the most part.

It's his brother's idea to outsource for assistance. Dansforth doesn't believe that it's healthy for Herbert to always be alone. He wanted someone working part-time to keep Herbert company. It took a little convincing on Dansforth's part. Eventually, Herbert agreed to this arrangement.

However, the difficult part is finding the right person, where personality types do not clash. After being interviewed for approximately twenty-five minutes, both Tollington brothers came to a unanimous decision. I am perfect for the job. Despite our age difference (Herbert at approximately 60 years of age), we seemed to have a lot in common.

During that initial introduction, I didn't realize the depth of and how many similarities we actually have.

Almost a family bond. What a bizarre feeling. Is it possible to forge kinship from oblivion? I just met the guy recently. Oh, well.

I'll write to you again soon,
Reinhardt

18ᵀᴴ Entry: Mischievous Deviants

Hola Diary,

My new gig with Herbert has been going well, but I still need to blow off some steam. Earlier in the week, Stephan and I went out to the city after hours. At night, we strolled down the street that was plunged in darkness, pouring bags of sugar into the gas tanks of parked cars. It's a classic prank and a goodie. I felt compelled to set one of the automobiles on fire, but Stephan wasn't in the mood for arson.

Last night, my brother insisted on going out to a nightclub. He told me that there is a slab of strange out there with his name on it. Honestly, what goes on in that deranged mind of his? Regardless, we dressed up for a night on the town. The time was 12:47 am.

My brother and I arrived fashionably late at Club Skeevies. I could hear the loud techno music blaring, even before entering the establishment. Once inside, the brief flashing lights caused me to become momentarily disoriented. This is not something I expected. I've been to nightclubs before.

If I suffered from epilepsy, I should've had a seizure long ago, and that has never occurred. Is it really much of a surprise that this music isn't to my liking? My appreciation of music extends to classical, not noise. Before long, I found myself at the bar, ordering a dirty martini. Stephan was already far from my sight.

With mild interest, I observed the other patrons gallivanting about. Dubious chatter is utilized once a male encounters his female prey. Probably fifteen minutes passed before boredom began to rear its ugly head. My current mood is not one for socializing in. Then it dawned on me that Stephan hasn't been seen in quite some time.

I began to search the premises, all the while wondering what he might be up to. His type of hijinks is the ones nightmares are made of. Eventually, I discovered a corridor that consisted of numerous doors. Behind one of them, a waking nightmare awaits. I tried turning each one of the knobs. Every room appeared to be occupied.

The exit door at the end of the hall leads to the alleyway. Muffled noise came from this door that had been left ajar. Subsequent to exiting the club, I discovered Stephan standing over a disheveled, half-beaten woman. They were in-between a couple of dumpsters. My brother's pants were around his ankles.

The unidentified victim was lying in refuse. Her dress was torn and bloody. She cried and whimpered as Stephan picked up her torn panties and threw them away. My brother pulled his pants up and greeted me with open arms.

"What the hell is going on here?" I asked.

Stephan stood there with hollow eyes and an expressionless gaze. Moments later, he awakened from his trance-like state.

"It's always the same. One way or another, I'm getting some strange," Stephan replied.

For the record, I do not condone this type of behavior. My brother and I have been bonding more so, exponentially, especially during the past week. Then he conducts himself in this manner. How shameful and utterly disappointing. Stephan sat down on top of the poor lass and strangled her.

Subsequent to the murder, Stephan required my assistance in picking up the woman and tossing her inside of the dumpster. After completing the callous deed, Stephan slammed the dumpster lid shut. My brother told me to never leave any witnesses or victims alive to testify. That's the easiest way to get caught.

Frankly, I was entirely apathetic regarding my brother's victim. However, when it comes to my own backside, I'm very much concerned. When I committed murder, there was a valid reason to do so. Gale threatened me with blackmail. On the other hand, Stephan created a predicament that shouldn't have existed in the first place.

I do not wish to spend my remaining days on earth cohabitating with cretins inside of a prison cell. We both walked calmly yet quickly out of the alleyway and down Foster St. This is where my car was parked. Hopefully, there aren't any witnesses to this abhorrent incident. Windows, a camera, one single bystander is all it takes to unravel the tapestry of my life. This simply will not do. Once the vehicle was located, we got inside of it and rode straight home.

I instructed Stephan to never speak of this. My brother simply laughed.

"What would I want to do that for? Besides, nothing happened in the first place," Stephan said.

Gwen sat in the den, patiently waiting for my return. Upon arrival, I embraced my lady love with a tight bear hug and the most passionate kiss. One for the ages. Gwen stared at me with sorrowful eyes. She deeply regretted her recent behavior.

My lady professed her undying love for me. If only her words rang true. Stephan entered the kitchen and made himself a sandwich. Apparently, sexual assault builds up one hell of an appetite. My concern is that if (more like, when) he does it again, I cannot be the least bit involved, even if it's only to assist with the clean-up work.

Why can't he have some normal bad habits like picking his nose, or not praising God before eating a meal at the dinner table? I'm only joshing. We're all atheists in this house. Praying on the premises is not sanctioned.

Hopefully, Stephan hasn't changed in that aspect. Otherwise, he would be one of the greatest hypocrites ever. Well... maybe not. Back to my relationship with Gwen. I know there is a bevy of things to work on, but we'll see it through.

Sometimes love isn't enough. It's the strive and dedication that will put us over the top. When a guy has a great gal, what more can you ask for? I'm certain that there are an abundance of methods and strategies, Gwen and I have failed to try yet. My time at work allows me a chance to contemplate our relationship and figure out what the best course of action truly is.

It's too bad that I cannot confide in Stephan regarding this matter. Clearly, he is incapable of comprehending a loving bond between partners. Nevertheless, it is very late at night with morning looming.

I'm going to carry Gwen upstairs. My lady has some new lingerie, she's been "dying" to show me. Ha, ha, ha. That one never gets old. Anyway, I can't wait to see it.

So, I'll be signing off for now. Resolutions will be discovered during these difficult times. I just know it. Look at me being so optimistic. It's better if I wake up from fantasy land.

Until next time,
Reinhardt

19ᴛʜ Entry: Couples Counseling

Bonjour Diary,

Do I seriously have to mention how lovely it is to have massive monetary means at my disposal? Money can give you access to almost anything that your heart desires. What I yearn for above all else is to save my flailing relationship. No, not really. That was a harsh exaggeration.

Things really aren't that bad. We just have a few issues to address. Due to the highly unorthodox circumstances surrounding my relationship, it is imperative that I hire a professional therapist who can keep his (or her) trap shut. The confidentiality clause of treatment must extend to the current status of every participant in therapy. If one of us is no longer among the living (so to speak) and the other is, that shouldn't impede the counselor's ability to assist patients.

I spoke to Marty the other day. He recommended Dr. Regivald Levy. This man is dedicated to helping couples overcome the insurmountable odds that have been stacked against them and obtaining the almighty dollar for himself. Levy's greed alone should guarantee his silence. In passing, it was also fair to mention that I keep a professional hit man on retainer. That way, he wouldn't get any cute ideas about reporting sensitive information to the authorities.

Yesterday was our first session with Dr. Levy. An aging avaricious man with salt-and-pepper hair. His glasses slid to the edge of his nose. He came to my home dressed casually, wearing a polo shirt and sweatpants. Does he believe that this is his day off? Is he about to go play golf?

This atrocity was committed in extremely bad taste. I wanted to crack Regivald's skull open then and there. Somehow, I manage to control my impulses.

The good doctor's jaw dropped when he laid eyes on Gwen. This is merely an introduction that I'm speaking of. At first, I thought this reaction was from feeling captivated by Gwen's impeccable beauty, but then I realized that this is far from the truth. In reality, Dr. Levy couldn't fathom my adoration for this lifeless corpse.

Regivald is not much different from the others, but he'll have to suffice. The session had taken place in the drawing room. Gwen and I each sat on opposite ends of the couch. Levy seated himself in a sofa chair, ten feet away. Of course, he faced forward in our direction.

A wide variety of questions were asked by the good doctor. First, Levy wanted to know how Gwen and I met. This is information that I refused to divulge, but I assured the man that it was truly love at first sight. As our session went on, I explained how I did everything possible to help with Gwen's personal aspirations. Her desire to become a professional photographer is hardly a secret.

Gwen had to realize that, due to her newfound disability (being deceased), this particular dream is no longer a realistic option that can be achieved. As an alternative, I simply suggested that the woman should get some work as a model. For such a gorgeous gal, this is not an unattainable task.

The good doctor asked Gwen what is it that she wanted out of life and death. My lady became unresponsive. She sat there with her mouth gaping open and flies buzzing about. I should've used mastic tape on this occasion in order to seal Gwen's mouth shut. Although, she wouldn't be able to provide feedback on important issues. Perhaps I'll have to install long bolts through the jawbone. I'll ask Marty for advice on this later. It might be about time to bring her in for maintenance anyway. Later during the session, Gwen decided to open up regarding her feelings. She stated that I was spending too much time with Stephan and Marty.

My priority has always been my relationship with Gwen. I couldn't believe what I was hearing. Then Gwen informed both me and the good doctor of her cooking endeavors. She admitted that her temperament has been out of sorts lately. My lady wished to be supportive of me as well.

This is why she's been learning a lot of recipes. Gwen thinks that the way to my heart is through my stomach. Her effort is appreciated. Suddenly, I excused myself then entered the kitchen. Returning only moments later, I had a platter in hand. After removing the cloche, I offered Dr. Levy some of Gwen's freshly baked vanilla lemon cake.

Regivald accepted my offer. The doctor reached out, but I pulled the platter back in protest. This did consist of a little teasing on my part. I placed the dish on top of the coffee table. Quickly, I had to acquire plates and utensils for everyone.

We're not going to eat with our bare hands. When did we all become barbarians? The doctor finally received an opportunity to try a piece of cake, as well as the rest of us. Simply put, it was divine. Pure ambrosia is what Dr. Levy is now privy to.

He did not hesitate to compliment Gwen on a job well done. Presently, my lady's head was tilted back, mouth still wide open, and a fly was crawling on her right eyeball. I utilized a swatter to get the little bugger. After killing it, I carefully used a napkin to clear away the remains from Gwen's eye.

Dr. Levy has been paid handsomely for his expertise as well as discretion. I can't help but acknowledge the fact that he tried his very best to appear as though Gwen's odor did not affect him. Another matter to discuss with Marty. I sprayed Gwen with an abundance of air freshener, which didn't make much of a difference. Then I returned to my seat.

We only had ten minutes left of this one-hour session. One matter that requires immediate attention is our love life. In that department, everything has gone fairly well. However, I did have an interest in spicing things up a little. When I spoke of this, Dr. Levy displayed an expression of bewilderment on his face.

As if he didn't know what I was talking about. The man began to sweat profusely. This isn't the time for a lack of candor. We were down to five minutes. The good doctor eventually spoke.

"Exploration in the intimate field is perfectly normal. A little experimentation might be good for both of you. In order to avoid a stagnant state, feel free to indulge in your innermost fantasies. If you remain open and honest with one another, this may very well lead to an overall improvement in your relationship," Dr. Levy said.

Before I realized it, time was up. The session had concluded. Did Gwen and I receive all of the answers and guidance we were searching for? Only time will tell.

Dr. Levy seemed extremely anxious. He was in a hurry to receive his payment and then leave. With haste, I wrote him a check. I graciously thanked the good doctor for his services and po-litely reminded him about the assassins that are kept on my payroll. Levy nodded his head. After receiving payment, he almost tripped over his own feet while fleeing from my abode. What a day of revelations.

Goodbye for now,
Reinhardt

20ᴛʜ Entry: Three's A Crowd

Buenos días Señor Diary,

Last night was quite the venture. Dr. Levy left a profound effect on me. So, I had to take his advice to heart. Let loose and allow the cards to fall where they may. Stephan accompanied me for another guy's night out.

This time, I had a premeditated motive. Part of my goal was for my brother to become so intoxicated, he would agree to come along with me to the graveyard after leaving the club. His assistance is necessary for exhuming another dead body. I didn't dare ask Marty. He already helped me once before.

Also, he's aware that Stephan is currently living with me. Why would I ask Marty to do such a thing if my brother is present? That is the reasoning that my oldest friend would use. Quite frankly, he'd have a valid point. Stephan doesn't contribute anything to the household.

He sleeps during the day and complains about Gwen's body odor whenever she's in the room with us. Usually Stephan wears a face mask to greatly reduce the stench that he's able to smell. Only a month has passed since Gwen's demise. I've been actively giving her injections of embalming fluid and storing her in extremely cool conditions. More permanent tactics must be deployed and soon.

Nevertheless, Gwen and I have decided to spice up our love life. We've agreed to engage in a menage a trois. It might be a little difficult to find a lady among the living who would participate in such an event of her own volition. So it becomes natural to seek out someone who is suffering from the same misfortune as Gwen. As such, she will not be the slightest judgmental.

My lady exudes excitement for meeting our new plaything for this evening. It is of the utmost importance that we get our relationship back on track by any means necessary. To be perfectly honest, I was just as excited as Gwen, perhaps more. As the meticulous man that I am, rushing without research is not in my DNA. Time had been utilized to carefully peruse the obituaries.

This particular encounter was designed as a means to an end. An activity that will take place only once. My intention is to find someone of the finest quality. Several candidates were discovered. All three of them had a similar build to Gwen. Their ages ranged from 28-36.

How utterly delightful. Attractive hens that are in dire need of being plucked. For the moment, Stephan must remain oblivious to my endeavors. He has to become inebriated in order for me to reason with him. Ultimately, Stephan will do my bidding.

Preparations for the evening were made. My brother and I decided to give our patronage to a different club this evening. A wise move considering that the last club we went to resulted in a homicide. Stephan gave me his word that he would behave as a gentleman instead of a ruffian. Of course, once the drinking has commenced, all prior good intentions start flying straight out of the window.

There we were in Club Harlot. A strange woman with a unibrow approached me. She attempted to engage me in mindless chatter. Wonderful... a bloody rambler. She continually talked without the slightest care that I didn't show any interest.

A single thought remained on my mind, the desire to take a straight razor and run it through the middle of that ghastly unibrow. If I were not gentle and took off a little flesh with the hair, so be it. Despite not currently having a straight razor in my possession, I was confident in my ability to find something sharp enough to get the job done. This is an outrage. How did this woman honestly expect someone to sit with her and stare at this hideous display? Sorry to say that her face, as a whole, is immensely unappealing.

Someone, anyone, should burn it with a flat iron and start again from the drawing board. Yes, I'm aware that's not how things work. She'll be damned with that face for all eternity. A fate worse than death. What an appalling appearance.

Her ensemble wasn't bad, overall. A cute orange blouse and blue miniskirt with matching shoes. She looked like a well-dressed wombat. Before long, my mindset had been altered. Visions of stomping in this rambler's skull flooded my head.

God, how she went on and on. What she's talking about, nobody knows. Will this garrulous creature's prattling ever cease? Didn't seem like it would. Should I take matters into my own hands and end her loathsome existence? No, I can't do that. I'm not a murderer. Well, technically, I am. Although it only happened once. I killed out of necessity. Doesn't this qualify?

Don't the masses deem it essential for this broad to shut the hell up? I glanced at my watch. Nearly thirty-five minutes have passed since this abomination entered my life. Where in the world is Stephan? I haven't seen him since our arrival.

With haste, I finally leaped up from my seat and rushed off in search of Stephan. I could hear that annoying harpy in the background, asking me where I'm going. If any part of me enjoyed killing, I could certainly have a good time causing her demise. There wasn't any sign of my brother. Then I decided to open the back door and take a peek.

I wondered if history is doomed to repeat itself. Soon I learned, indeed it is. After going outside, I walked halfway down the alleyway. Muffled cries and grunting came from behind one of the dumpsters. The son-of-a-bitch (Yes, I'm aware that we have the same mother) was at it again.

I caught Stephan in the middle of the act. He saw me, then asked if I wanted a piece. How barbaric as well as reprehensible. It's unbelievable that this grotesque reprobate and I share the same gene pool. After climaxing, he reached into his pocket and pulled out a straight razor (Damn, where was that when I needed it?)

Stephan almost slit the woman's throat. This time, I intervened, but not out of the goodness of my heart. I told my brother not to make a bloody mess and to strangle the woman just like last time. Stephan shrugged his shoulders before putting the straight razor away. Then he promptly engaged in choking his victim.

It didn't take long for this woman's struggling to cease. Her final breath has been taken. I instructed Stephan to wait there until I bring the car around. He asked me what I had in mind. A response was not given.

I had to move quickly to acquire my vehicle. After running ragged and out of breath, two minutes later, I returned with the car. At that time, Stephan was informed that his latest victim was coming with us. As the body was loaded into the trunk, I glanced at Stephan with the realization that at times, his dastardly deeds can carry some degree of merit. Luckily, there weren't any pedestrians roaming about that could grace us with their presence.

During the ride home, I asked Stephan for the lady's name. It happens to be Cheryl.

Until next time,
Reinhardt

21ˢᵗ Entry: Time For Some Action

Hey there Diary,

I wanted to write more during my last entry, but there were things I had to address elsewhere. Where did I leave off? So, after my brother and I arrived home with Cheryl, it was time for a meet and greet. I introduced the newcomer to my lady love. Merrily, Gwen and Cheryl became acquainted.

I insisted that Stephan needed to grab a wash towel and clean out Cheryl's vagina properly. I didn't want this woman to contain any semen from the previous occupant. Stephan complied with my request. He realized that his promise to me had been broken. However, my brother is oblivious to the fact that I actually benefit from this outcome.

The inconvenience of having to exhume a recently deceased human being from her grave has been thwarted. Three days of recovery time were required after the last exhumation. My body ached and throbbed with pain. So much digging in a relatively short amount of time. I accomplished more than Marty, but it wasn't his cross to bear.

It's only right that the majority of this burden should fall on my shoulders. Also, it doesn't hurt that Cheryl is just as attractive as her buried competition. Those ladies will remain where they are. Sleep tight tonight!

However, back to last night's event. Stephan must've been all tuckered out from raping, because he went straight to bed. Gwen eagerly awaited my grand entrance into the bedroom with our new friend. We were still on the first floor. I dragged Cheryl by her legs. Her head hit every single step on the way up.

Fortunately, she won't need aspirin for any impending headaches. I suppose that's one advantage to being dead. When I entered the bedroom with Cheryl in my arms, Gwen became extremely excited. She was positioned on the bed with her legs crossed. A sheer beige piece of lingerie is what Gwen wore. Dainty little thing.

Fatigue caught up with me, so I plopped Cheryl down on the bed. After undressing both Cheryl and myself, I realized that some excrement had seeped out from the confines of Cheryl's rectum. The mess was combined with a little urine that also managed to make its way out. Quickly, I pulled Cheryl off the bed and into the bathroom to address the matter. No one I know of can engage in sodomy and enjoy it while their penis is submerged in fecal matter.

Soon enough, Cheryl's naughty parts were properly cleaned and sterilized. We returned to bed at once, after dimming the lights in order to create a more suitable setting. There was so much passionate kissing between us all before Cheryl decided to perform fellatio on me. This is when Gwen took some initiative and sat on my face.

Our sexual escapades continued onward for quite some time. Once all of our most intimate desires were fulfilled, I kicked Cheryl out of bed. Gwen and I spooned just a little longer. Eventually, I got dressed and dragged Cheryl downstairs. We entered one of the bathrooms, where I had already prepared the necessary tools.

It's not that Cheryl didn't have any value, but I already have a girl. Perhaps she'll meet the right man in the afterlife. With the lady now inside the bathtub, I used my trusty hacksaw to carve the night away. This is a brand new one. If this were a rusty hacksaw, this job would become much more difficult to accomplish.

If Stephan taught me anything, it's that you must take your time to cut up a cadaver properly.

Once the deed had been completed, I was able to fill eight trash bags with Cheryl. I just don't have my brother's patience. Larger pieces of the deceased were still intact. Don't worry, I double-bagged her.

Cheryl's remains were packed into the back of my truck. I returned to Drakken Lake with a play-mate for Gale. I'm glad that she'll finally have some company out here. Unless the rumors of an exist-ing alligator within the vicinity are true. It might've fed on Gale's remains already.

It's doubtful that there are really any gators around here. While riding in a canoe, I lowered one trash bag after another into that dark, murky void. The water was blacker than the night. People don't typically come out here to fish. This is why I believe that dumping victims into this particular lake is my most optimal choice.

After completing the task, I drove home in a hurry. All remains have been discarded, but I still didn't want to get pulled over by the patrolman. My vehicle's speed was gradually reduced. Vigi-lance must be maintained. Finally, I made it home just before daylight.

Probably twenty minutes after my arrival, dawn was upon us. Preparations for bed were made, then I dove underneath the covers. It felt good to snuggle up with Gwen. This entire experi-ence taught me that I didn't require another woman to satisfy my needs. Everything I find alluring in life is right here by my side.

Fortunately, Gwen feels the same way. What an extremely long night. Perhaps I overexerted myself. Felt like I could sleep for two days straight. Never take a good woman for granted.

I immensely appreciate everything that Gwen provides me with. Her love is untainted. Am I falling in love all over again? There isn't anything that I wouldn't do for her. Gwen gladly reciprocates this sentiment.

My true love is what this darling angel will always be. I made plans for Wednesday. Marty and I will be meeting. This time, I will be accompanied by Gwen. A sustainable alternative for my lady's longevity must be explored. Marty has agreed to try what should've been done in the first place.

His taxidermy skills will be fully utilized and put to the test. This procedure, being conducted on a human being, is considered by most as highly immoral. Thank goodness this taxidermist couldn't care less about people's morality and standards of this supposedly evolved civilization. Are these guidelines and principles set in stone by God? There are so many different gods that the masses believe in.

An abundance of religions exist. Regarding this subject, the difference between the right and wrong one is conjecture. Who really knows which god truly exists, and what this celestial being believes? Is there one at all?

Marty is a man of science. Biology, to be exact. This is something that we have in common. His knowledge and skill set can lead to an eternal union between me and Gwen. Everlasting love is the greatest gift of all.

See you next time, Diary
Reinhardt

22ND ENTRY: A MOST GRUELING PROCESS

Dear Diary,

I bore witness to an extraordinary act of preservation. Such an astounding feat, and I have Marty to thank. At first, it didn't seem feasible. Embalming fluid can only get you so far. Gwen has been deteriorating. Slowly but surely.

It became more than obvious that my lady love is decomposing at a more accelerated pace. I had to act fast. Stephan decided to come along for the ride. Subsequent to arriving at Marty's funeral home, he instructed us to bring Gwen into the prep room. All of her clothing had to be removed.

The stench of Gwen's corpse had reached a whole new plateau. An alarming problem that also required a solution. Marty had a small, steel medical cart that was covered with surgical tools. All of the living wore masks. Stephan stated that he's willing to participate if the situation calls for it.

We laid Gwen on top of the long steel table that was located in the center of this room. Wide empty containers were on the floor, within close proximity. Martin Furhnam is quite skilled at what he does. The work is intense and strenuous. Not an easy task to complete by any means.

First, most of Gwen's major organs needed to be removed. Scooping out 20 ft. of intestines is an exhausting task on its own. An unraveled slippery hose with much more to come. Yes, Marty, free my lady from the stifling bondage of entrails. A surgical drill was utilized to help crack open the cranium. The brain had to go as well. With Marty's magic involved, the top part of the skull had to be reattached.

He made the skull appear as though it had never been breached. Gwen's oozing eyeballs were exchanged for acrylic artificial implants. A dazzling pair of unblinking wonder. What a sight to behold. These appear to be organic and more durable in the long run. So many integral details that must be observed and taken care of. The expertise of my dear friend is a godsend.

After Marty cleared out as much of the body's interior matter as possible, he began to fill the nearly vacant cavities with excelsior. Plaster cloth had been layered all around Gwen's limbs. Typically, very little could be done regarding the maggots that were being produced inside of Gwen's corpse, exponentially. However, Marty has always been one for innovation. He utilized a machine that had a fairly thin tube attached.

It had a mechanism that produced a vacuum suction. This tool was used for the inside of every orifice in Gwen's body. Then, a molding plaster became most beneficial. Marty created cul-de-sacs that were set deep down inside each orifice to reduce the amount of maggots that would come forth. A sheer protective material was perfectly bound to various body parts.

So much vital work in the hands of one man. Can't help but express my admiration. At long last, the procedure has been completed. Next, my beloved was given a sponge bath, then makeup was applied. Before long, Gwen 2.0 was ready to emerge from the ashes, anew.

She could not be back in my loving arms soon enough, and then I saw her. How can this be? Is it possible that this astonishing creature is even more breathtaking than before? Stephan, Marty, myself included, we all removed our masks. I swear it's my imagination.

Did the putrid odor that Gwen always emitted finally dissipate? A second opinion was required. I asked Marty for his input. Perhaps, I've become far too accustomed to the smell. My dear friend told me that the repugnant odor has indeed vanished.

Stephan also shared this sentiment. Today is the day of miracles. After dressing Gwen, I lifted her up with glee. To my surprise, Gwen is so much lighter than before. Apparently, excising vital organs from one's body is essential for significant weight loss.

Gwen's entire skeleton, which is still intact, helped to prevent her from floating away. I'm ecstatic that for the very first time, Gwen's natural musk will no longer act as a distraction from my innate loving ways. In celebration of my lady's liberation, I invited Marty back to my place for a night of drinks and debauchery. We didn't currently know of any ladies to invite for this sordid soiree, so I called in a couple of professionals. Their tasks were to entertain Marty and Stephan.

Regarding my brother, I explained that the woman for him has already been paid. Therefore, you cannot rape a willing participant. Not to mention, I paid using my credit card. If any harm were to come to these women, then we're all going to jail. Stephan gave me his word that he would be on his best behavior.

At this juncture, Stephan's word means less to me than dog excrement. However, under the circumstances, I was fairly confident that he could get through the night without committing a felony. Subsequent to arriving home, I presented the men with alcohol. Bottles of scotch, whiskey, and bourbon were placed on the countertop of my bar, which is located in the den. I didn't dream of pulling out the quality liquor.

Fine wine is too good for my guests. No offense to Marty, but he doesn't know what fine wine is. As for Stephan, he's a lush. He'll drink anything that is placed in front of him.

In addition, there are the ladies. Is it necessary for me to comment on them? They are prostitutes. High-class escorts, but nevertheless... Speaking of the devil, almost an hour had passed since placing the order. Finally, these gorgeous ladies of the night arrived.

Both of the women were dressed to impress. They wore tight mini dresses, stockings, and shoes of high-caliber brands. One woman was wrapped in a mink stole. Stephan was in the mood for Indian tonight, so I hope he eats well. Marty requested a Russian girl.

I didn't know what his endgame was, but far be it for me to ask questions regarding his personal preferences. Of course, I was accompanied by

Gwen. The woman who sat with Gwen couldn't just have her drink in silence. She became inquisitive and asked if Gwen was alright. In addition, she added that Gwen appeared to be a little glassy-eyed.

Stephan told her to shut the fuck up and finish her drink. This type of speech is rather uncouth, but I certainly didn't blame Stephan for it. I felt very much like saying something similar. The woman didn't utter another word about Gwen. It can be said that overall, everyone had a delightful time.

Gwen and I are deeper in love than ever before. Who could ask for anything more?

Until we meet again,
Reinhardt

23RD ENTRY: THE RIGHT ARM OF THE LAW

Dear Diary,

I am compelled to ask, what is the law? What is it good for? Absolutely nothing. Gale Whitherspoon her disappearance is hardly a tragedy. A nuisance whose entire existence baffles me. No one misses her, nor should they.

How dare that callous cow make an attempt to blackmail me? She isn't worth the dirt that I step in. Diary, you might be wondering why I would dredge up unpleasantries of this caliber. The answer lies with my most recent visitor. Earlier this afternoon, there was a knock on my door. With reluctance, I answered it.

It happened to be Deputy Patrick Hendsworth. A most intrusive little prick. I attended high school with the bugger. He stood at about 5'11. Red-headed devil with a beard.

Look at him, walking tall with his shitty beige uniform. A silver star pinned to his chest like a goddamn merit badge. Should've polished it fifty more times. It looked like he missed a spot. I haven't seen him in years.

We were never friends. Back in school, he was the dweeb that everybody picked on. I never indulged in the shenanigans because my time was better spent planning experiments on animal carcasses. Apparently, Deputy Hendsworth finds self-worth in displaying authority over other people. Somehow, Pat felt that this choice in life compensated for his lack of manhood.

He's been in law enforcement for probably the last fifteen years. The officer had a medium build, which I found shocking. I expected so many years of shoving donuts down his throat on a daily basis to result in immeasurable weight gain. What did I owe this displeasure? Big man on campus.

All pedestrians must take heed when crossing the street. This sour puss will give you a ticket for jaywalking if he catches you. Deputy Hendsworth stated that he had an important matter to discuss with me and wished to come inside. Personally, I detested the notion of this peon entering my homestead. I couldn't stand him back in high school, and think even less of him now (If such a thing is possible). Despite my inner feelings, I allowed this dismal human being to come inside.

It's best not to make myself look suspicious and appear as an extremely cooperative citizen. Besides, Marty is at his own home. Stephan is out somewhere, gallivanting, and my beloved is upstairs in bed, resting. I invited Pat into the drawing room, where we could both sit and talk. Although, I expected this to be more of an interrogation than a pleasant chat.

Typically, I would offer a guest some coffee or tea, but I did not wish for Hendsworth to overstay his welcome. Not to mention, he wasn't welcomed in the first place. I will try my best to recollect a few details from that dreaded discussion.

"Are you acquainted with Gale Whitherspoon? Deputy Hendsworth asked.

"Only mildly," I replied. "She was a recurrent customer of mine. My former profession in the food delivery industry caused our paths to cross on a multitude of occasions."

This inquisition carried on for about twenty minutes. Gale has been reported missing. Apparently, the woman used that big mouth of hers to inform her roommate of a little crush that she had. Unfortunately, it was on me. Demanding legal representation before answering any additional queries could draw forth much more suspicion. Therefore, I reluctantly remained cooperative.

Deputy Hendsworth only interviewed me because my limited association with the deceased had been revealed. Without witnesses or a body, the authorities will not attempt to bring forth any charges against me. Suddenly, Stephan walked through the front door as the officer was leaving. Hendsworth asked my brother a few questions before departing. The deputy seemed to be quite satisfied with our responses.

He got inside his patrol car and sped off after receiving an urgent call on his radio. An ample amount of relief eased away the tension. Stephan asked if I had considered eliminating the deputy. I told him no. As long as they never find the body, there aren't any reasons to fret.

What a coincidence. Stephan just returned from Drakken Lake. He had a last-minute rendezvous with an unsuspecting hitchhiker. It's sad to say that she's no longer among the living. I'll cry later. The more important thing is that while Stephan was in a boat dumping the body overboard, he caught a glimpse of the long-rumored alligator that inhabits the lake. In fact, after Stephan rowed back to shore, he spotted a second gator. Who knows how many are out there? The most vital takeaway from all of this is that these apex predators have most likely been feeding on the remains of our victims. Hallelujah! Praise, Jesus! I'm still an atheist!

Stephan and I gave each other high fives and embraced in a hug. It's as if we had access to the Everglades, but we don't live anywhere near Florida. On one side, those cadavers will never be discovered, and they'll never receive the proper burials that they deserve. However, there is a silver lining here. Stephan and I will be getting away with murder scot-free.

We can thank wildlife preservation organizational efforts for this. In celebration of this superlative news, I treated Stephan to a glass of Nieport. A very fine tawny port, indeed. From 1912, I believe.

Naturally, I imbibed slowly, appreciating that subtle but present caramel flavor. A hint of smoked almond, perhaps. It is always obligatory that the bottle is allowed to breathe before one partakes in consumption. On the contrary, Stephan guzzled his glass of wine as if it were fruit punch. I quickly presented my brother with a low-grade of scotch.

He can't tell the difference, and couldn't care less. As long as the liquor imbibed caused Stephan to become inebriated, then the mission has been accomplished. After a while, I ascended upstairs with my port and two wine glasses. Why would Gwen be left out of the festivities? These are the moments we must treasure.

I'm not going to jail, and my brother... will continue to do the same shit over and over again. It's inherent for him to do so, I suppose. Before long, Gwen requested a third glass of wine. What a naughty girl. Clearly, she was in the mood.

I didn't hesitate to pull a black gimp mask over my face and howl at the moon. Life is good.

Until next time,
Reinhardt

24ᵀᴴ Entry: Revelations Of The Nefarious

Dear Diary,

A short time ago, I finished my shift. Attending to Herbert is hardly a stressful task, because for the most part, he can take care of himself. Most people would describe him as an ornery old cuss that's not long for this world. Personally, I refer to him as a delight. Today, he granted me with so much wealth in knowledge.

Herbert always felt that there was something about me. He could see it in my eyes. Over the last several weeks that I worked for Herbert, he became comfortable enough to divulge little secrets with me regarding his past. Perhaps it was a recognition of kindred, like-minded beings that both bathe in the same cesspool called life.

During Herbert's early adulthood, he helped to manufacture mannequins of various types. His creations were shipped to department stores all across the nation.

Some even made their way overseas. The Europeans seemed to enjoy his work immensely, as additional products in higher quantities were requested over the years. However, the creation of dummies was far from being Herbert's only occupation. Have you ever heard of The Highlight Killer? This particular murderer operated during the 1990s.

He would record the death and mutilation of his victims. Then he'd leave a videotape that contained the highlights, near the corpse. These tapes were deliberately left behind for the police to obtain. All across America, The Highlight Killer would leave his calling card. The authorities failed in apprehending the culprit responsible for taking so many lives.

Then, over the hush of static from his old TV set, Herbert leaned in. With a tone that was almost casual, he uttered the words that made the air freeze: 'I was the Highlight Killer." He also told me that if I ever consider turning him in, nobody will believe me. Why in the hell would I do such a thing? To be perfectly candid, I felt a little insulted that Herbert could think so little of me. So, I decided to express my thoughts to the man.

After I responded to the confession, Tollington made it clear that he didn't really think that I would squeal. Otherwise, he wouldn't have shared such intimate information. I can also recall his words vividly.

"I know what you are. You and you're brother. The apple doesn't fall far from the tree. It makes so much sense because your father was the same. A dear friend of mine.

We were practically brothers. However, Dansforth did not approve of our association. An extremely intuitive lad. He knew that your father was pure evil. Droff was only a few years older, but he taught me everything I ever needed to know about murder. After all, he was the master," Herbert said.

This brings us to my lineage. Before now, I've never discussed my parents. In particular, my father, one of the most dreaded serial killers of all time known as Times Two. He had an affinity for showing off. His modus operandi was to kill no less than two people at a time.

During this period, if the police only found a single corpse, then it's guaranteed that my father didn't commit the murder. There are cases where the culprit responsible could've been The Highlight Killer, since he was my father's protégé. Who really knows for sure? On occasion, Herbert and my father would coordinate. Although, my father had a much higher body count.

According to reported accounts, Tollington killed nineteen people. The fact that Herbert never reached that coveted milestone of twenty murders drove Herbert crazy. On the other hand, Times Two slaughtered sixty-four victims. At least that's the confirmed tally on file. It is believed that my father's body count could possibly be over a hundred.

The D.A. offered him a plea deal. Confess to and reveal the whereabouts of missing victims and receive a life sentence without the possibility of parole. Times Two refused the state's generous offer. He wouldn't give the D.A. the satisfaction. The case went to trial, and my father received the death penalty.

He sat on death row until his appeals finally ran out. Twelve years later, the nefarious Two Times died in the electric chair. Before the switch was pulled, my father spoke his final words.

"Sheriff Cenpold, I want you to light up my life!" Times Two exclaimed.

My mother, Margaret, was a delusional woman who couldn't cope. She told reporters that it
wasn't his fault. Her husband worked hard during
the week and just needed to blow off a little steam.

After Times Two's conviction, my mother blew
her brains out with a service revolver. Stephan and
I were only kids at this juncture. So, we were sent
to live with our grandparents. An absolute tragedy
that made the headlines. My mother could always
see the good in people, even if they were complete
monsters.

My father treated her well. He saved all of
his pent-up aggression for his victims. Personally, I
could never see myself killing innocent bystanders
for sport. If I were to murder someone it should be
in the name of self-defense, survival, they laughed
at me, or looked at me funny... Oh, my.

Murdering as a form of thrill seeking is something that clearly appeals to Stephan in abundance. However, I always thought I was immune
to whatever this sensation is that causes people
like my father and Stephan to kill at will. There is
a subtle progression in which I find homicide more
appealing than ever. Regardless, I do have more in
common with my mother. She could never muti-
late people for self-gratification.

I consider a loving relationship to be much
more enticing, and I mustn't do anything to jeop-

ardize that, including going to prison. My father, Belial Droff, was a demon in human form. His reign of terror came to an end many years ago, but my brother and I are his legacy. It came to my attention that Stephan has a staggering body count himself. I asked him about it, and he didn't mince words.

He confessed that he's responsible for the deaths of twenty-one women and two men. Truly a chip off the old block. My father would be so proud. No, I'm not being facetious either. A world where we can present ourselves uninhibited and exposed in full form, true and unbiased. That's a paradiso that I want to live in.

Unfortunately, this is not the realm known as reality. Everything that I just described is rooted in fantasy land. Herbert's profound revelations left an invisible mark, and I thank him for it. Far be it to hide in the shadows. Be true to thyself.

Stephan doesn't suppress his intentions. If he is intrinsically bound to rape women, so be it! Actually, that part is rather awful. If he enjoys strangling women, so be it! (That's much better.)

As for me, love is my guiding light, and I cannot contain it any longer. Tomorrow night, Gwen and I are going for a night out. This dead woman and I are deeply in love, and the entire world should know! Well, no. Attention should not be brought to the authorities.

We'll go out while being subtle and discreet. At least I'll genuinely try. Look out, world, here we come. I'd better go now. It's time to lather Gwen up with baby oil.

I'll write again soon, Diary,
Reinhardt

25TH Entry: Is This Really Happening?

Good morning, Diary

I had a late, venturous night filled with excitement. Where do I begin? Gwen wished to look her best for our outing. She wore elegant evening wear. A fire-red dress with matching heels. The diamond bracelet that I gave her is a spectacular accessory.

A hairdresser was called in today to take care of Gwen at my home. (Someone who is guaranteed to keep her mouth shut) Working diligently with delicate precision, her eyes never dared to meet mine. My lady's hair was set with long, lustrious curls. A radiant sight that is capable of blinding me with her unparalleled beauty. I wore a suit and loafers (no tie). After combing my hair and a splash of cologne, Gwen and I were ready to embark on an excursion of fun.

A limousine ride had been arranged for this evening's affair. Rufus is my requested driver from a well-established service that I frequent. He always remembers that discretion is the name of the game, especially with a $100 tip. Cours is a city located forty miles away. We had an early start.

I've been there twice before in the past. The downtown scene at night is spectacular. There are so many activities to engage in. Once we arrived, the first stop on our itinerary was to see a play. It is entitled: Kiss My Hairy Bum.

A performance of comedic variety. I read that it has received superlative reviews. Gwen has quite the funny bone. She loves to laugh. Personally, I prefer something with a more dramatic flair, but the experience is for Gwen's benefit. Whatever my lady's heart desires.

Once we entered the theatre, we received a bevy of odd stares. Cold gazes accompanied by cringing. Radiance of our standards can give pause to those that are sullen with envy. What, they never saw a man drag a woman closely by his side? After passing through the vestibule, a portly onsite manager asked if my lady was alright. I assured the meddling prick that Gwen is perfectly fine, and that she just had a little too much to drink. Before the fat bastard could utter another word, I slipped a $50 bill into his hand.

"Please enjoy the show," the manager said.

Gwen and I hurried to our seats. The show commenced five minutes later. In retrospective, even with the intermission, those were a difficult three hours to get through. Gwen actually enjoyed the production. She laughed and laughed.

I'm glad that my lovely lady was satisfied. As for myself, the poorly written script with juvenile humor is beneath me. Someone, anyone, should set fire to the theatre and teach them a lesson. No one deserves to ever be exposed to such mindless drivel. I was in the mood for a cocktail.

We left the theatre, then our chauffeur drove us to the Lipstick Dipstick Lounge. After approaching one of the unoccupied tables, I pulled a chair out for Gwen. She thanked me while sitting down. I used my handkerchief to dust crumbs and other debris away from my seat before sitting directly across from Gwen. The place itself is a small, cozy dive.

Lights were deliberately dimmed throughout the establishment. The reduced amount of illumination is used to create an intimate and relaxing atmosphere. There certainly wasn't any shortage of patronage. So many people were talking at a high volume. Desperately attempting to hear themselves over others. I found this most disconcerting. The amount of noise undermined the prospect of decompressing. Prolonging our stay at this establishment is not ideal. A single drink will suffice. A server came by to take our order.

I instructed her to bring each of us a martini, extra dry, and not to forget the olives. There appeared to be many lesbians who drank in this lounge. Several of these women were checking out my lady. This display caused me to chuckle. If they only knew.

Most living humans are not into dead people, women or men. Perhaps the heavy eyeliner and blue eye shadow were a bit too much for Gwen, with her lips laced with a hot pink color. Maybe my gal did look slightly slutty, but I consider her much more mesmerizing than all of the carpet munchers that surrounded us. Gwen is a ravishing woman. Part of me wanted to take her right then and there.

Although I haven't completely lost my mind, have I? Those looming lustful thoughts soon dissipated. Not a moment too soon. Gwen began to receive more unwanted glances. Suddenly, I realized that Gwen was hunched over, hanging halfway out of her seat.

With haste, I got up and positioned her upright and properly. The server returned with our drinks. The ogling from the other patrons finally ceased. Gwen seemed much more relaxed than I. She was having a lovely time.

My lady doesn't go out much, so the least that I can do is provide her with a worthwhile experience. Soon we finished our drinks. Gwen wished to request another, but I insisted that we take our leave. I didn't appreciate all of the attention that Gwen had garnered earlier on. We made our departure without incident.

Then Rufus drove us to the Chey Kitty Club. My lady and I spent a couple of hours inside, just burning up the dance floor. I prefer a more sophisticated classical playlist of music. Perhaps that fifth glass of wine had affected me. As house music blared from the speakers, it became apparent that Gwen had some remarkable dance moves.

The way she can contort her body is spellbinding. Being completely devoid of innards must give way to a tremendous amount of flexibility. This should be duly noted for later tonight. Could I possibly be inebriated at this point? Of course I was. Gwen's love is intoxicating. There isn't anything in the world like it. Now, at one o'clock in the morning, we must flee this place. After returning to the car, I instructed Rufus to bring us to Rackshire Park. A lovely, quaint little place on the outskirts of town.

Upon our arrival, I vacated the vehicle with my beloved. The two of us made our way to the pavilion. Gwen sat on top of the table that was located in the center of the structure. Stars throughout the sky were shining bright. The air was cool and soothing.

It had been a magical night for the ages. I must've spent ten minutes straight telling Gwen what she means to me, and explaining that my life would be quite minuscule in scope without her. My desire is to never wake without Gwen by my side. Nervously, I reached into my pocket after getting down on one knee. I presented my lady with a gorgeous 2-carat diamond ring.

I asked for Gwen's hand in marriage. She smiled while accepting my proposal. After engaging in a kiss, I forced the ring onto the finger of my beloved without tearing too much flesh. Apparently, the ring was smaller than I thought. A little repair work on Gwen is now required. All will be done in due time. Is anything ever easy?

That's all for now,
Reinhardt

26ᵀᴴ Entry: The Clique

My dearest Diary,

The upcoming nuptials between my fiancé and me are a glorious miracle in the making. For the first time ever, I think that I've been exposed to some degree of happiness. What an odd feeling. It certainly isn't a bad one. Now I see why it's such a sought-after emotion. Strange to reach such a plateau of bliss, never before imaginable during my life time.

Don't think that I'm neglecting you, Diary. A couple of weeks have passed since my last entry. I've been extraordinarily preoccupied. My fiancé has been busy coordinating with the wedding planner. Of course, my presence is necessary to help facilitate the process of conveying any points that Gwen wishes to express.

Marty and Stephan, along with myself, have become closer than ever. A true camaraderie has formed between us. I'll always be grateful for the opportunity of meeting the dreaded Highlight Killer a.k.a. Herbert Tollington. He became the mentor that I never requested. He continues to enthrall me with his tales of serial murder.

The man is filled with such passion when he relays these stories of yesteryear. Much to my delight, Herbert always kept a copy of every murder that he ever filmed. Always one videotape left behind to taunt the police, and a copy is kept for posterity. Herbert has accumulated many of his souvenir tapes throughout the years. Similar to my father, The Highlight Killer's body count is significantly higher than what the authorities suspect.

Numerous boxes inside Herbert's home were filled with evidence. It is never advisable for a serial killer to keep mementos of his crimes. Herbert told me that at the time he had become so overconfident in never getting caught, his natural instincts were ignored. Feeling like a god, Herbert wanted something that he could treasure while reminiscing over his victims, which is so sweet when you think about it. Upon our first meeting, I would've never taken Herbert as the sentimental type.

You can learn something new about a person every day. My job detail requires nothing more than keeping Herbert company. It doesn't feel much like work at all. I get paid handsomely for spending time with a great mentor and friend. I have to admit that the more tales of homicide that Herbert spews, the more my bloodlust increases.

Doesn't mean that I'll act on such urges without a purpose. However, I might be inclined to murder if given half the chance. What does that say about myself, or the company I keep? Tollington is a retired serial killer. Stephan is a relentless rapist.

Then there is Marty. He is aware of everything that we've done. Both my dear friend and Stephan met Herbert's acquaintance. They all have bonded as well. Stephan was more than pleased to discuss our father's illicit hobbies.

My brother and I were lied to during our entire childhood regarding who are father really was. This is truly a travesty. Our grandparents were only doing what they felt was best. However, I certainly don't agree with that erroneous decision. Neither does Stephan.

In particular, my brother seems to have required a renewed sense of pride regarding our notorious father. Up until our teens, we were told that he died in an electrical wiring accident, and our mother mistakenly mishandled a firearm. It was a delight to learn from my father's apprentice what a night on the prowl was really like. On the other hand, Marty Furhnam doesn't come from such an esteemed lineage. His family was comprised of simple people.

Running a funeral home business is an outstanding trade. The remarkable skills Marty has honed under proper tutelage have helped me out of a bind on more than one occasion. This man's talent isn't anything to scoff at. Most ordinary humans would define Marty as a morbid, soul sucking undertaker that only comes to life when he has an opportunity to sleep with someone.

One day, we were alone, and the words came forth.

"Have you ever killed anyone?" I asked.

Marty chuckled at the thought.

"No, I haven't. But I'm not opposed to the concept," Marty replied.

Hearing that response from my best friend made me realize that maybe there's a potential killer lurking within the subconscious of every being. Could this possibly be true? Then again, we might just be a mass collective of psychotics that should be locked away in padded rooms somewhere. No, of course not. Men like us are meant to roam free.

We are highly evolved creatures. Everyone else is sheep, and they're only good for one thing:

to be slaughtered. Oh, my. These must be Herbert's words seeping into my subconscious. Some form of subliminal programming. I do regard mankind itself as a pestilence that should be eradicated from the face of the earth.

Only a chosen few should be exempt from such a fate. Of course, such a list would include yours truly. Somehow, I feel as though life for me has just recently begun. Things have gone splendidly well as of late. As the inherent pessimist that I am, one can only conclude that less-than-appealing occurrences are looming.

However, with my bride-to-be, her exuberance is flowing from her like lava. She already ordered the perfect dress. Invitations have been circulating among the public, including several of the surrounding communities. Come one, come all. Other than the people within my own clique, I don't have anyone else to invite that I am actually fond of.

Gwen doesn't have any family to speak of. Although, I do have a special surprise in store. Well, I'd better get back to it. So many tasks at hand, and not a moment to waste. You'll learn everything soon enough.

Until then,
Reinhardt

27th Entry: The Day Of Reckoning

Greetings and salutations Diary,

The day we've all been waiting for has finally arrived. After giving an incredibly generous donation to a particular church, I was able to reserve not a small but a gargantuan chapel in size. It's located in the quaint town of Dunsky. The wedding had a massive turnout. Apparently, these greedy vultures found the concept of free food and drinks most appealing.

Was it an error in judgment to invite these random orangutans to such a prestigious event? Short answer is no. There is a method to my madness. Beggars can't be choosers, or can they? Some of these people are mild-mannered, middle-class individuals who actually possess a strain of proper decorum.

Others seemed to be of a lower class. A few of them behaved just as well as the pillars of society. Then there were the ruffians and scallywags. I can't imagine what rock they crawled out from under, but here they are in the flesh. I'm certain that the only reason there was such an enormous turnout is due to the advertised free buffet.

These vultures will have their fill, but little do they know that the main course will be something far more... Unexpected. Stephan, Marty, and Herbert Tollington were all in attendance. They all had parts to play. My brother decided to step aside and allow Marty to be my best man.

The acquisition of this role became most appealing to my dear friend. Six women were hired as the bridesmaids. Each of them wore hideous, matching light green dresses. Not that my bride-to-be had any competition from these ladies, but if she did, no one could tell while laying eyes on that repulsive attire. The priest, Kip Nachen, finally arrived, only slightly inebriated.

He kept a flask in his back pocket. An occasional swig was taken now and again, just to settle his nerves. There must've been over a hundred guests. These people do not have any shame. Very few attendees congratulated me on my upcoming nuptials.

The bulk of this mass eagerly anticipated the end of this sacred ceremony before it even began, because they were all aware that only at this time, everybody will gain access to the free food, desserts, and beverages. Every one of these rapacious leeches should be condemned to an eternity in the roasting pit of Hades. Goddamn them all! Nevertheless, the time had come for the ceremony to commence. Stephan locked the main entrance doors. He implemented the use of chains to keep the strays away.

No one else is permitted to invade the church during this majestic union. Almost all of the guests were seated. The benches were filled to capacity. Organ music began to play. Stephan walked alongside me.

I traversed the aisle, thinking to myself that the devil will have his due. Once I stepped in front of the altar, Stephan took a seat. Marty stood close by. My mind began to focus on the love of my life and the rapture that she will provide. Many people were complaining about the occupants who sat in the first row of the bride's side.

I gave forth a valiant effort to ignore them. Suddenly, the rear doors opened wide. Gwen appeared wearing the most radiant white dress. She gleamed in beauty, similar to a diamond without flaws. Herbert escorted her down the aisle.

This was a difficult task for the old man because he walked with a cane. Therefore, he didn't have any other choice but to drag her along. Bewildered looks appeared on many faces throughout the chapel. A sense of shock is a strong feeling that permeated this crowd. Once Herbert reached the altar, I presented Gwen with a surprise.

"Look, Darling, in the front row! Your parents couldn't make it because they're still alive, but we exhumed your grandparents! Surprise!!" I exclaimed.

An abundance of these fools who attended my wedding gasped in horror. What little do they know of love. I thought a tear nearly fell from Gwen's eye. She was overwhelmed with joy. The skeletons of my lady's grandparents were well-dressed.

However, the couple seemed to be in desperate need of getting some sun. Their bones seemed a little bleached and pale. Spending years underground can have that effect. The preacher began to speak. Gwen and I turned to face one another.

Marty helped to hold Gwen in place. We declared our vows, then Marty handed the rings to me. An exchange of jewelry was conducted between me and my bride. Tedious line after line spewed from the preacher's mouth. If anyone had an objection to this union, they would've been flatlined instantly.

Fortunately, none of the vermin were foolish enough to oppose my will.

The priest sighed, "I now pronounce you man and wife. You may now kiss the bride," he said.

After a lengthy embrace and passionate kiss, my wife threw her bouquet. No one caught it. In fact, women attempted to avoid it. The flowers landed on the floor. There weren't any cheers to speak of. Although members of my entourage applauded.

Then I began to French kiss Gwen. Worms are beginning to form inside her head again. I accidentally swallowed a few. The guests were instructed to follow Marty into the grand hall, which is devoid of pews. In this area, food is served.

My stomach turned as I observed those gluttonous pigs chowing down. Gwen sat in the other room next to her grandparents, getting reacquainted. At this time, I opened a large crate, located in the corner. Marty, Stephan, and Herbert approached me with much enthusiasm. It had to be as previously discussed.

The four of us were entitled to engage in some friendly hijinks. This day will truly become one to remember for the rest of our lives. The crate was filled with some extraordinary treasure.

Herbert chose the machine gun. Marty picked up the chainsaw.

Finally, Stephan made up his mind. Blow torch it is. As for me, I found the pickaxe most appealing.

"Gentlemen, have at it. Remember the rules: No survivors," I said.

Stephan quickly gave an elderly woman a new hairdo after setting her head on fire. People began to scream at the top of their lungs. As far as I'm concerned, they deserved to die just for being loud and disruptive. An old man was sitting alone and eating cake. Marty revved up the chainsaw and cut the old codger in half. I assume that the gentleman will not be having seconds.

Herbert's aim isn't what it used to be. Without hesitation, he gleefully dispensed bullets into the crowd with a sunny disposition. What kind of marriage celebration would it be if I didn't partake in the festivities myself? Every human cranium I cracked wide open with my precious pickaxe caused me to feel tremendous gratification. A strong sense of achievement was felt by ending the lives of undesirables.

Believe me, there were many worthy candidates. Due to all doors of the church being locked with chains for reinforcement, none of the guests were able to survive. Although it wasn't from a lack of trying. Some of the victims attempted to do more than simply run away. They actually had the audacity to fight back, but it was all for naught.

One after another, they met their demise. Salvation can only materialize in the form of escape. Therefore, only damnation exists on this phenomenal day. At one point, while my cohorts remained immersed in bloody carnage, my new bride pulled me aside. She looked deep into my eyes and held my hand tight.

Gwen told me that her second chance for happiness in the afterlife wouldn't have come to fruition if it weren't for me. These words that were uttered from my blushing yet pale bride truly instilled me with much optimism and hope for the future. There isn't a doubt in my mind that with Gwen by my side, the world has become a vast vessel of opportunity. Love will show us the way.

Signing off now,
Reinhardt

EPILOGUE: 28TH ENTRY

Dear Diary,

Remember me? It's been so long since my last entry. That was well over four years ago. Allow me to bring you up to date. There were consequences for The Wedding Day Massacre. This is how the public has labeled the glorious event.

On that faithful day, the police finally arrived at the church. By then, every single one of those guests had been slaughtered. If you're going to be that late, why show up at all? Herbert Tollington screamed at the cops and told them that they'll never take him alive. My dear mentor blew his own brains out with a machine gun.

I was taken into custody with Stephan and Marty. Thanks to a lack of witnesses, we were easily able to convince the authorities that Herbert was solely responsible for all of the bloodshed.

For the old man to be given so much credit... He would've wanted it that way. Marty and Stephan were released from custody soon after the initial interrogation.

Two years ago, my brother was arrested and charged with sexual assault. His victim managed to survive the ordeal and testify in a court of law. There was also an existence of physical evidence. Stephan was found guilty in a court of law. He is currently serving a ten-year sentence. A cruel, perverse fiend, yet I care for him nevertheless.

Marty continues to work at his own funeral parlor. He has become quite prosperous. Thanks to the carnage at my wedding, my best friend has gained an infinite amount of clientele along with some national notoriety. As for myself, when the police learned of my unorthodox marriage to a cadaver, I was immediately admitted to the Black Heart Psychiatric Hospital. They finally released me yesterday.

Gwen's remains were returned to their original resting place, subsequent to being discovered at the church. More recently, they were retrieved. It pays to have friends of high quality. As a welcome home gift, Marty exhumed Gwen's corpse. Oh, how I missed my loving wife. I longed for her with each passing night.

Now I'm back home with my beloved spouse, whom I cherish like a crown jewel. I've begun to peruse the obituaries. There have been quite a few stillborn fetuses buried recently. Gwen and I both agree that this is optimal timing for us to start a family. Then I came across a news article regarding a newborn infant (only three months old) that died from SIDS.

A beautiful baby girl. This prized candidate is perfect. I'd better go load the shovels into the truck now. It's always a pleasure to share with you, Diary.

Truly yours,
Reinhardt

ABOUT THE AUTHOR

Sean Seville is an author/entertainer from Chicago, Illinois.